TRAPPED

TRAPPED

Nowhere, USA Book Three

NINIE HAMMON

STERLING & STONE

Chapter One

Stuart McClintock got no warning. He was driving down a winding mountain road about to cross into Nower County, Kentucky, when the road in front of him exploded.

KaBoom!

Blew up!

The sound was defeating and the slap of concussion that struck his car just about put him in the ditch.

And it was the road that blew up. Not something *on* the road because there was *nothing on the road*. There were no cars ahead of him, had hardly been any traffic at all since he got off the interstate. And he had not met a single car, pickup truck, cattle truck or rickshaw coming his way in the past half hour.

It was the road itself that blew up, like there was a landmine under the pavement.

Stuart hadn't been going fast, unaccustomed as he was to driving on mountain roads like these, so when he laid on the brake, the sudden stop didn't send him plummeting over an embankment and off into *nowhere*.

The squalling protest of screeching tires filled his ears and the smell of burning rubber filled his nostrils.

When the car finally came to a complete stop, he settled back into the seat, might have bruises from where he'd slammed into the seatbelt harness that had kept him from flying through the windshield. He'd turned off the driver's side airbag when he got into the car — was skittish about an accidental ignition in a car he wasn't familiar with. Maybe that'd been a mistake.

He sat for a moment, his heart hammering a hole in his chest as he watched the plume of dirt, hunks of asphalt, and rocks begin to settle slowly back down to earth.

Was this some kind of missile? From a rocket-launcher of some kind? Artillery fire from … where? Fort Knox? He wasn't completely sure where Fort Knox was, except that it was near Louisville — which was hundreds of miles away. He'd taken the ridiculously early flight out of Chicago into Lexington instead of Louisville this morning for that very reason, and though he wasn't completely certain of the gold depository's location in relation to where he was now sitting, he was reasonably certain that a misfire from one of their howitzers would not make it all the way into the Appalachian Mountains of Eastern Kentucky.

Mortar fire? He supposed it was possible. He had not served in the military, so had no point of reference except the movies — somebody yelling "incoming round" followed by an explosion. Was this the kind of hole a mortar shell made?

Who'd be firing a mortar at an empty road?

What if he'd been going faster? If he'd been even a few seconds farther down the road he would have been sitting on top of the asphalt as it was launched up into the stratosphere.

Was that it?

He began to look around apprehensively. Was somebody trying to blow up a car on the road, saw him coming and set off the charge too soon? Not him specifically. How could he possibly be a target? He'd never met a living soul from Nower County, Kentucky except Charlie. Unless she'd put out a hit on him — and he supposed, given the circumstances, that was indeed possible — nobody even knew he was coming.

So an attempt to blow up a random car was the only logical explanation. Who'd do a thing like that? There were multitudes of idiot lowlifes who got their jollies by throwing things off bridges at random cars below.

This could be that. Except it couldn't.

Bridge dumpers likely put no more thought and foresight into their mayhem than, "Hey ... wanna drop a rock on a car? Heh, heh, heh." It required no greater sophistication than the ability to open their fingers and let go of a rock and no grander tools than the aforementioned rock.

Whoever did this planned it. This was a purposeful act by somebody who appeared to know his way around an explosive device.

Stuart yanked open his car door and got out, but just stood there by the door, ready to make a hasty retreat if one seemed warranted. There was no vehicle on the road beyond the gaping hole in the asphalt. And he could see nobody — wait, there was a guy standing there on the other side of the hole! How had he not noticed the guy before? He was just standing there all by himself, no vehicle, and he seemed to be as surprised to see Stuart as Stuart was to see him.

The guy was big, lumberjack big, square jaw, blunt features, rugged. Somebody you'd want to have on your side in a bar fight. He had black hair with a white streak like lightning had struck him in the head and left its mark.

Dressed in bib overalls with a white tee underneath like maybe he'd just walked off the set of *Deliverance*.

How had Stuart only just now noticed that the guy was standing there a little way beyond the haze of settling dirt and dust? He must have been there all along, had to have been, so why didn't Stuart notice him before?

The guy smiled, looked like he was just about to lift his hand and wave, and then he lowered it slowly, like his inclination to be friendly had suddenly and completely left him. His smile drained off his face, and what it left behind was not an expressionless face. He looked confused and then frightened. Frightened turned to scared, scared turned into terrified and the man suddenly whirled around and bolted down the middle of the road, just ran blindly away from the hole in what five minutes ago had been solid asphalt.

The man stumbled over his own feet and fell, immediately rolled over onto his back and rose up on his elbows. His features were blurred by the haze of dust still lingering in the air. Even so, it was impossible to mistake the look of horrified terror there.

He screamed. A sound that Stuart would forever remember as the sound of sheets ripping. It was too high-pitched for a man and yet it matched the look on the guy's face. The scream went on and on, he appeared to be cowering away from something that was hanging above him. Except there wasn't anything hanging over him.

Then the thing happened that couldn't have happened but did. The man appeared to be in *a circle of reality that was … shrinking.* Like Stuart was looking at him through the closing aperture on a camera, which didn't open and close like a door but regulated light by making a circular opening wider or closing the circle so small it was only a pin hole.

The circle of reality around the man shrank smaller and smaller.

The sheet-ripping screech the man had been wailing suddenly cut off, as abrupt as turning the handle on a water spigot.

That was because the circle around the man who'd been making the sound had closed up around him and he had … *vanished.*

Where'd he go? The guy, the one in the road …? Where'd he go?

Stuart literally rubbed his eyes, blinked to clear them, but he couldn't manage to do anything to make the man … be there.

He'd been lying in the middle of the road and then …

That was cra—!

How could that—?

What was going on here?

Stuart found himself running though he didn't register anywhere in the higher centers of his brain either the decision to do it or the will to carry it out. He was just running, sprinting to the edge of the … the crater in the road and climbing down into it. The rift stretched in a jagged line from one shoulder of the road to the other, a hole four feet deep, though it had been filled back in to some extent by the cascade of rocks, dirt and chunks of asphalt raining out of the sky.

He clambered over the rocks, heedless of his expensive Italian shoes that had definitely not been designed for such usage. He stumbled, scrambling up out of the hole, went down on one knee and snagged a small rip in his suit pants.

Staggering out over the debris of asphalt chunks and rocks on the pavement beyond the hole, he raced to the spot where the guy …

There was no guy.

Stuart looked around, turned 360 degrees, shading his eyes and looking off into the distance.

Where did he go?

There was not so much as a stand of tall grass anywhere around, and even if the dude could do a hundred meters in under the world record thirteen seconds, he could only have made it to the bushes growing alongside the woods and they weren't thick enough to hide in.

This was nuts!

Where. Did. He. *Go?*

Stuart got down low on the spot where the guy'd been lying, looking for … he didn't know what. Some trace that less than sixty seconds ago a man had been lying in this exact spot … and then he wasn't.

Magic happened all the time in Charlie's children's books, but this was real life, not fantasy. In real life, people didn't just … vanish.

But this guy had.

Which could not possibly be true. And that could mean only one thing—

Ever rational, logical Stuart McClintock: If he's not here now, and there's nowhere he could have gone, then he was never really here at all. Stuart had imagined him.

That was the only logical conclusion to come to, the only reasonable explanation. Only it was a pile of the warm sticky substance you find on the south side of a horse going north.

Stuart was *not* imagining things. There had been a man standing there. Stuart had seen him, could describe him, all the way down to the white streak in his black hair.

Okay, he was here. Then where'd he go?

Stuart looked around one final time, like maybe the

guy was hiding under a rock and Stuart just hadn't noticed—

The guy hadn't been there at first.

Now Stuart's heart kicked into a full gallop.

That's right. When Stuart first looked up after he stopped the car, looked through the falling debris, there had been nobody on the other side of the road. No car, no truck, no person. The road had been empty.

And then the guy appeared and Stuart just assumed the guy'd been there all along and he just hadn't noticed him, but when he replayed the surveillance cameras in his brain, there was no sign of anybody on the other side of the road in the beginning.

Now he was getting somewhere. Not only did the man vanish in a puff of smoke — almost literally — but he'd appeared out of one, too.

Appeared. Then vanished.

For one brief, hysterical moment Stuart wondered if they still put crazy people in straitjackets.

Don't cinch the belts too tight on him, boys, wouldn't want to wrinkle his suit.

He shook it off, reoriented himself.

Reality check. Somebody had blown a hole in a state road, made it impassable. Needed to get a state road crew out here to put up sawhorses, barriers, or somebody either entering or leaving Nower County was likely to run off into …

The hole in the road was on the county line.

Maybe right smack in the middle of it.

So what did that have to do with anything?

"Done!" He said the word out loud. A verbal acknowledgement that he was not going to chase these lunatic notions around and around in his head. He had better — *more important* things to do.

And now, on top of the other things he had to do, was the added task of going around this hole in the road. He'd have to find another way to get to 2811 Barber's Mill Road. He'd picked up a new Kentucky map at that gas station off the interstate. When he'd asked for a map of Nower County and the guy had looked at him like he'd grown a third eye.

"I never had anybody ask me for a map of Nower County. The folks who live there don't need one, and don't nobody else ever go there."

Stuart turned back toward his car on the other side of the hole and noticed the sign set back from the side of the road. What with one thing and another — explosions and magical vanishing people, stuff like that — he hadn't thought to look for what Charlie'd told him about it.

It was just like she'd described it. On an old, dilapidated sign were the words "WELCOME TO NOWER COUNTY." But somebody had added letters to the sign with red paint, crudely drawn but definitely readable. There was an "H" between the "W" and the "E" and an additional "E" added to the end of the word. Making Nower County Now**h**ere County.

After he'd studied the sign for a moment he looked around, and was mildly creeped out by how quiet and empty it felt here, all by himself with no other cars on the road.

He was suddenly in something of a hurry to climb back across the crack in the road and back into his rented red Lexus so he could pull the map out of the glove box and chart a route to Charlie's mother's house, different from her simplistic description of how to get there. *It's at the foot of Little Bear Mountain, on Barber's Mill Road. Just ask anybody.*

When he was finally behind the wheel again, he pulled

out the map, acknowledging as he did so that he and the map would soon be engaged in mortal combat — Stuart trying to fold it back the way it had been, and the map resisting every such attempt.

He traced with his finger the interstate south and east from Lexington, but after that he got confused by the smaller roads ...

Then he noticed it.

County lines and names were in gray superimposed on the topography, and the space occupied by Nower County was visible — between Drayton and Beaufort and Crawford counties. But the name wasn't there. "Nower County" wasn't on the map.

Chapter Two

If it hadn't been for little Cody, Shepherd Clayton would have lost his mind, gone completely insane. They'd a had to haul him off to the looney bin in chains.

His baby son needed him and that kept him going, from one minute to the next. Without that need to hold himself together, Shep woulda fallen apart. He wasn't strong as Abby, not near as strong as Abby and without her by his side …

After a while, he couldn't even decide anymore what was the craziest — what had happened or that didn't nobody care what had happened.

He and Cody'd waited at the hospital all that morning for Abby to come and get them. Had it been two weeks ago? How could it have been two weeks? It had, though. Felt like just yesterday that he'd been eager to see his wife pick up their baby son, snuggle him and nurse him. She'd been so excited. They'd been feeding him her breast milk, but from bottles 'cause he was so little and weak at first he couldn't nurse. Before they took him home, she was gonna nurse him for real for the first time.

They'd waited. And waited.

Truth be told, Shep was stunned she'd been able to stay away as long as she had. It'd taken every bit of arm-twisting he could apply to get her to go home for one night, just one night, to rest up before she was up and down at all hours feeding the baby. Abby didn't even know how puny she'd got since Cody was born. She hadn't never been bigger'n a minute and after she had such a hard pregnancy, she'd fallen off to near nothing. Clothes just hung on her.

But what he'd seen then had made him love her even more'n he did, and she was the only girl he had ever in his life cared about. When she got down so skinny, staying by that baby's side in the hospital neonatal care unit, refusing to leave except to go to the bathroom, eat a sandwich or a candy bar when Shep could stuff it down her. All her attention was focused on Cody.

What he seen then was like them things he'd seen on television once — fiberoptic cables. Just strands of pure bright light. That was Abby. Everything else was gone and she was just pure light.

He knew soon's she got him home she'd hover over that baby night and day and he wanted her to get one night of rest, just one night of uninterrupted sleep *in a bed* — she'd slept sitting up in a chair for months. A good night of sleep would give her some strength for what was coming.

They hadn't had time to do much of anything after Abby found out she was pregnant. She got that pre-eclampsia and was so sick she had to stay in bed and then Cody'd come early. From the moment she went into labor and they headed off to Lexington so scared couldn't either one of them hardly breathe, she never set foot back in their house in Poorfolk Hollow. That'd been months ago. He figured it'd do her good to put up them pictures — little kids with great big eyes — her sister'd had on the wall in Wally's room when he was a baby. Couldn't put much on Cody's wall 'cause the room was so little — they called it a nursery but it wasn't really nothing but a walk-in closet.

They didn't have no proper baby bed, but Abby'd fixed up a little cardboard box with blankets and it'd suit just fine.

Even so, Shep figured she'd go home and get that room ready and then she would drive on back to Lexington, not even stay the night 'cause she didn't want to be away.

He'd been proud of her that she had done the smart thing, got herself some rest, was gonna come all full of energy and love and … and …

She'd told him she'd be there in time so's she could feed the baby before they went home. She wanted to nurse him his first time there, where the neonatal nurses would be around to help out and … mostly just to cheer her on.

When the morning come full on and she wasn't there yet, he figured she'd either got stuck in traffic — Abby wasn't used to driving in the big city — or she'd had car trouble. That poor old truck was like to fall apart any second. Assorted members of Shep's huge family had come up to Lexington to be there to welcome Cody and Abby when they wheeled the two of them out to the car. They'd all stayed at his brother's house so there'd be plenty of folks to go get her soon's she called and said where she'd broke down.

But she didn't call.

And she didn't come.

When the nurse come in and said they's gonna have to go ahead and feed Cody because he was crying real hard, Shep'd knowed right then in his gut that something was wrong. Bad wrong.

By noon, he was so frantic he couldn't sit still. They'd

tried to call the neighbors and her sisters and brother to see if they knew where she was but something was wrong with the phones. They just rang but didn't nobody answer.

They checked Cody out and Shep rode in the front of his brother Roger's truck, holdin' that baby — they was gonna get a carseat and all that, but right now — kept his head ducked down kinda covered up in the baby's blankets so his brother wouldn't see that he was crying.

When they turned off Sawmill Lane onto that little road that didn't have no name where their house was …

Everything after that was crazy jumbled up in Shep's head and he couldn't sort it out now, figure out what had happened when.

He remembered scraps of it pretty well — remembered his mama holding Cody, standing by the front of Roger's truck while Shep screamed and kicked in the back door of somebody's black Ford Tempo. He didn't know whose it was. He didn't remember nothing about the Kentucky State Police, but somebody said they'd called them. Said they come and looked and took down stuff on forms on a clipboard and said they'd get right on it.

Didn't nothing come of it, though.

He remembered his mama setting him down in that old rocking chair on her porch that had a view back into Nower County from Flatrock Ridge in Beaufort County. She'd handed him Cody and told him — with tears in her eyes — that he had to look after his baby son best as he could and the whole family would help.

He sat there and rocked, just rocked. He didn't seem to be able to think what to do so they all told him he needed to eat, or sleep — but he didn't do neither one of them. Mostly, he just held Cody, fed him when his mama give him a warmed-up bottle of formula that didn't set well with the little fella's stomach and he puked up most of it.

Didn't matter no more that Shep didn't go to work. They'd laid him off, said it wasn't the same as firing him but it still meant he didn't have no job. Not that he could blame them — they was work to be done and Shep wasn't never there when he was supposed to be to do it.

It wasn't until he went over to his and Abby's house, made himself go, that a tiny thread of sense began to pull free of the insanity. Went by himself 'cause he didn't have no idea how he was gonna respond to it or what he might do and he didn't want nobody around to see. What he done was just sit there. Didn't cry nor scream nor talk … didn't even think, really. He just sat there. And once he'd got real quiet, he seen how quiet the place was. A funny kind of quiet that wasn't hollow sounding like most quiet. Echo-y like, the way the church building sounded when you was the last one to leave and you cut off the lights and walked up the aisle through the sanctuary in the dark. That silence sounded big and empty.

The silence in his house where his wife and baby son was supposed to be but wasn't, was not empty silence. It was full, swollen silence. Silence stretched so tight over sound that it was bulging out on all the sides, about to pop.

You could put your ear up to that kind of silence and if you's real quiet, you could hear the sounds in the silence. No, on the other side of the silence. The voices. Whispering.

The whispers sounded like the not-sound of sand blowing across rocks. Or death beetles scrambling, scarabs they was called.

And after a while, Shep got where he could pick out one voice in particular in all the whispers. Abby's.

Chapter Three

Even after almost ten days of rehearsals, Stuart McClintock still didn't know what he would say when he saw his wife, only that it would most certainly *not* be, "No, wait, please … I can explain." He didn't want to sound like a B movie. And he really *could* explain. Just had to get Charlie to hold still, stop exploding all over the place long enough to listen to him

Charlie had mentioned once that finding her mother's house was easy, as finding mountain houses went. The road from Lexington was County Road 278 East. Just stay on it until you hit the road her mother's house was on — Barber's Mill Road — and turn right. Now that he couldn't stay on one main road, he'd have to cobble together a meandering route down one tiny road after another running roughly parallel, the best he could tell, to the county road.

Half a mile later he was totally lost.

How did these people ever figure out where they were going on all the winding, twisting mountain roads — most of which had no road signs, by the way? He wondered if that was chance or intentional.

During World War II, the British got their hands on Hitler's land invasion plan for England and it called for dropping paratroopers onto three "downs" — British for meadows — around London. So the people near those places changed all the road signs. The signs pointed to Somewhere, This Place, That Place, Another Place Altogether. Maybe these mountain people took down the signs because they figured that the people who lived here didn't need signs to tell them where they were going and people who didn't live here needed to go on back where they'd come from and leave them alone.

More likely, the signs just got knocked/shot off at some time in the past quarter of a century and nobody'd ever bothered to put them back up. Charlie had told him how "nowhere people," the residents of Nower County, felt about it — that the only good view of it was in the rearview mirror. He was sure they had their reasons, but he certainly didn't share that sentiment! Stuart thought the mountains, though maddeningly confusing, were stunning, breathtakingly gorgeous. If there were any way for outsiders to get here … to *find* here, this place could be turned into a tourist attraction for weekend getaways for city dwellers in five states.

Of course, that wouldn't work because the people of Nower County — *Nowhere* County — wouldn't welcome strangers with open arms. Charlie'd told him about that, too, how the isolation of the mountains had bred a clannishness that had to be seen to be believed, and a distrust of any and everybody who couldn't trace their Kentucky ancestry back at least three generations.

He finally found a little road that lead into Nower County called Blandford Lane. The first paved road —

there were several gravel tracks — that branched off
Blandford Lane was called — duh — Blandford Branch
and it led in the direction he thought he was supposed to
be going. (Just *don't* turn off Blandford Branch onto
Gopher Hill Road because it dead-ends, just *stops* at a creek
where once there'd been a bridge, though nothing
remained but hunks of concrete and rusty metal.) Beyond
Gopher Hill Road, Blandford Branch ended at another
road with a sign that was so full of bullet holes it was
unreadable. He flipped a mental coin and chose a left turn
on that road which led him to a road that *did* have a sign
identifying bullet-hole road as Byrne Lane and the cross
road as Sander's Lane which was something approaching a
"real road" by Stuart's definition, one the state road crews
might consider essential enough to plow when the snow
fell.

Seriously? What was he thinking? He'd bet his whole
stock portfolio that none of the roads in Nowhere County
ever got plowed, no matter how essential they were.

A randomly selected right turn on Sander's Lane led to
an underpass beneath what was probably a no-kidding, for-
real "main road," but there was no access to it.

He had not seen a human being since he had crossed
over into Nower County so the "just ask anybody" part of
Charlie's description of where her mother lived certainly
wouldn't have worked for Stuart today.

No human beings, but a plethora of wildlife. Deer
wandered out onto the road and instead of the proverbial
deer-in-the-headlights terror, they held their heads high in
a haughty challenge. *Hey, Bub, I live here. You don't. I'll thank
you to slow down. You might hit me.*

He saw other furry critters that he thought might have
been woodchucks, weasels or badgers — he didn't know
the difference — and a gaggle of wild turkeys (was gaggle

the collective noun for *wild* turkeys?). He had smelled a skunk, though gratefully he hadn't caught sight of it.

City boy that he was, Stuart would have been delighted and charmed by the flora and fauna if his gut hadn't been tied in such a knot of apprehension he was having trouble sitting up straight in the seat.

He passed a gravel track on the left with a crude hand-lettered sign nailed to a tree that read "Little Bear Mountain Sawmill."

Charlie's mother lived at the foot of Little Bear Mountain, and when the next crossroads — complete with sign! — announced that the road was Barber's Mill Road, he turned left toward the mountain. The house couldn't be far now, around the next bend, or the next — and even after all this time, Stuart didn't have any idea what he was going to say to her.

What would Stuart do if Charlie wasn't here?

Of course she was here. Where else would she be?

Then why hadn't she returned the rental car to the agency at the Lexington Airport? Or at least called to report that she'd be keeping it for an extra amount of time? That made no sense.

Neither did missing calls with her publisher. The two combined had lit a fire under Stuart, propelled him to Kentucky to find her. And tell her something besides "no, please wait … I can explain."

And he *could* explain. There *really was* a reasonable, not-break-up-a-marriage explanation for what Charlie thought she had discovered that had sent her literally "running home to Mama's." Well, to Mama's *house*. Her mother had died two months ago and Charlie'd been saying she needed to schedule a trip to Kentucky to "tie up the loose ends of her mother's life."

His two-week trip to Seattle had ended up taking

almost three, and he'd called her about his delay. She didn't pick up, or return his messages, but that wasn't strange. When Charlie got *in the zone* writing, she fell into a deep hole of creativity and pulled the dirt in after her. She hardly ate or slept and didn't interact with anybody other than the nanny who kept Merrie out of her hair. She had explained it to him:

"When I'm writing, there's a movie going on in front of my face and I have to type as fast as I can to write down all that I see."

Interruptions of any kind shattered the movie — a phone call, a doorbell, anything that broke her concentration. She said she could literally see the movie disintegrate. Like it was put together out of an infinite number of pieces of stained glass and the pieces clattered to the ground.

So he'd done what he always did when he traveled. He called and left her messages telling her he loved her, missed her, couldn't wait to see her — but didn't *disturb* her, showed respect for her creative process.

It did strike him as a little odd that the last couple of days before he came home, he had tried to leave a message on the answering machine, but couldn't — it clicked like it did when it was full. How could it be full if Charlie'd been listening to the messages every day and erasing them?

But he had blown that off.

He'd walked into their house in pristine Clarendon Hills, the tiny village west of Chicago that was the first small town Stuart had ever lived in, expecting Merrie's exuberant welcome and to sweep Charlie up into his arms in greeting.

Not. The house had been empty. He found a note on the dining room table beside a credit card statement with charges for plane tickets, a hotel room and meals in Hawaii circled in red with the pen Charlie used to edit her manuscripts.

"I know. I called the hotel in Oahu. Merrie and I are in Kentucky settling my mother's affairs. You need to be moved out before we get back."

He'd been totally flabbergasted, sickened when he realized that the note had been lying on that table for days. Which meant Charlie had spent all that time thinking he had been in Hawaii playing bump and tickle instead of negotiating a corporate merger in Seattle.

He called her mother's house. And called. And called.

The phone just rang — not even an answering machine where he could leave a message.

If his law firm hadn't been putting the final bow on the three weeks of work in Seattle, he'd have hopped a plane and flown to Kentucky the day he found the note. That's what he *should* have done! But at the time, he'd believed — *stupidly* — that since he really could explain the misunderstanding, all he had to do was *talk* to her …

Then came yesterday's back-to-back phone calls, a one-two punch to the chin.

One was a call from her publisher asking where Charlie was. She'd missed two conference calls about her upcoming book. The publisher had sent her the cover design — and Charlie was a fanatic about how her book covers ought to look — and had gotten no response. Hot on the heels of that call was the one from the Avis Car Rental Agency in the Lexington Regional Airport in Lexington, Kentucky. They were looking for Charlie, too, because she had rented a Chrysler Cirrus early Friday morning, June 2, and was supposed to return it by 5 p.m. Saturday. Neither the car nor Charlie ever showed up. They had tried to get in touch with her, but the phone number she had left merely rang and rang and nobody ever picked up. Exactly how they had tracked Stuart down was unclear, but what they wanted wasn't. He was to produce the car forthwith or ... followed by threats of legal action. He'd hung up before they really got rolling on that part.

After that call, he'd felt a chill down his spine, like somebody had poured ice water down the back of his shirt and it was slowly dripping from one vertebra to the next. He wasn't the kind of man who had a sense about things. He'd known them and read about them, people who said after a tragedy, "I just had a feeling something bad had happened." Stuart never had such feelings. He was a no-nonsense (Charlie referred to him as a "git-er done") kind of man who either never had such intuitions or had so successfully tuned them out for his whole life that he couldn't hear them anymore.

But he'd sensed something ominous then that he couldn't shrug off and had booked a red-eye flight out of Chicago to Lexington, with the awful "something's wrong, very wrong" feeling chewing at him like a lazy rat eating his guts. When he arrived, he spoke with the Avis agent who absolutely remembered Charlie and her "*precious* little girl." Clearly, the agent fell into Charlie's category of "everybody else." That's how Charlie referred to some people's responses to Merrie's obvious mixed-race heritage. There was "us" — people who didn't even notice and people who noticed but didn't care, and "everybody else" — people who noticed, did care, but pasted a smile on their mugs like a stick-on name tag and pretended they didn't.

Of course, Stuart had dealt with racism in all its myriad forms his whole life, though his 'famous football player" status had mitigated all but the most blatant forms of it in recent years. He'd grown a thick skin, no sense ...

what was it Charlie always said, "getting your panties in a wad" over it. But Charlie's panties stayed wadded up much more than his — because she hadn't had a lifetime to learn how to deal with it and because it was directed at her little girl, and Charlie would leap across a table and rip your face off if you threatened her child.

The Avis agent wanted him to hang around to talk to the manager about the rental car that had not been returned, and Stuart didn't have time for that, gave them a credit card number and told them to do whatever they wanted with it — charge on it the days the car had been gone past its due date, and all applicable late fees, of course — and if that didn't suit, they could charge him the price of the car and he'd buy the thing. He didn't care which.

He'd rented his Lexus from Hertz.

Rounding a spectacular hairpin turn, the road straightened slightly and Stuart saw a house ahead on the left. He didn't have to see the number on the mailbox. He knew it was the house where Charlie had grown up. From the handful of references Charlie had made to her childhood he had formed a mental picture of the place and this was it. He pulled into the driveway and parked. The Chrysler Cirrus Charlie had rented from Avis at the Lexington Airport was nowhere in sight.

He turned off the ignition and sat for a moment staring at the house. And he was afraid. Not concerned. Not apprehensive. Not worried or anxious, or uneasy.

Afraid.

Suddenly, Stuart McClintock was scared to death and he had absolutely no idea why.

Chapter Four

Cotton Jackson came upon looters on Main Street in Persimmon Ridge early that Saturday morning and didn't have any idea what he ought to do about it. Gratefully, they saved him the trouble of doing anything at all by taking one look at him, leaping into their pickup truck and hauling butt out of town, left a box of tools they'd been stealing sitting on the sidewalk in front of Peetree's Hardware Store.

It was bound to happen sooner or later.

They'd be back tonight or tomorrow or whenever. Once they bragged to their friends about it, wouldn't be long before all the businesses in town, in all of the towns in Nowhere County, would be stripped bare of whatever was on the walls there — because that's all that was left. Everything else was ... *gone.* Absurdly, ridiculously, *impossibly gone.* Vacant buildings, homes, the courthouse. Like they'd all been emptied out of everything so they could be repainted and the painters didn't want to chance a drip on the owner's belongings. Except the furniture wasn't sitting outside, waiting to be moved back in. It was ... gone.

When Lester Peetree had closed his little hardware store in Twig years ago and opened a bigger one in the Ridge, his son Willie had lined the walls of it with tools so customers could wander among them and pick out just the hammer or screwdriver or drill bit they needed. The tools were still there — or had been until looters came to steal them — but nothing else was left in the store.

Nothing was left in the parking lot out back, either. No cargo van with Peetree's Hardware Store stenciled on the side. Cotton hadn't seen a single vehicle of any kind — car, pickup truck, motorcycle, jeep, four-wheeler, tractor … golf cart or Sherman tank — anywhere in the county. The parking lots, driveways, garages and carports were as empty as the buildings.

And some of the buildings weren't just empty. Some of them had become dilapidated husks overnight, with sagging roofs, peeling paint, rotted boards. Every day there were more and more of those. Stores and homes all over the county. Cotton didn't know which frightened him the most, made him more nauseous — empty houses where the folks living there might have stepped out on the porch to watch the sunset or catch fireflies with the kids, or fall-ing-down shells, shacks that looked a hundred years old.

A hundred years ago would be 1895. Did that mean something? Cotton had no idea. He wondered, though …

Like he wondered about everything else in his life, had been wondering ever since the world as he knew it was shattered, the day everything he believed about reality and the whole nature of the universe crumbled at his feet. The day the world went mad.

Normal, garden-variety day. He'd stayed overnight in Lexington, slept on the lumpy cot in the employees' break-room at Polanski's Sewing Machine factory, where he was the production foreman, because he had stayed late to repair a broken piece of machinery and would have to be at work early the next morning.

Oh, how he wished he hadn't stayed, wished he'd gone home.

Right, stack that wish up on top of the pile of them that was topping out now at about the same height as the World Trade Center in New York.

Wished he'd gone home.

Wished he'd been there when whatever happened happened.

Wished he could have stopped it, or fixed it or ... or been there with Thelma at the end.

Wished he could peck his sweet wife on the cheek just one more time and pinch her butt and have her jump like she wasn't expecting it.

Wished he could figure out what catastrophic event had occurred in Nower County, Kentucky on June 3, 1995.

Wished he could find all the people who were missing.

Wished he could convince somebody — *anybody!* — that it mattered.

At age sixty-four, Cotton Jackson was a man comfortable in his own skin. He knew who he was, what he was about, and spent his days being grateful for all the good in his life. An eternal optimist. Thelma'd said he reminded her of that grinning sun on the box of kiddie cereal he always bought. He maintained that he was a simple life form — an amoeba in a world of multicelled fungi or bacteria or viruses or whatever was the next rung up on the evolutionary ladder.

Born in Nower County, married his high school sweetheart. Yeah, she was six feet two inches tall and he was five feet eleven inches and there were men that would have bothered but Cotton Jackson wasn't one of them.

They'd had Billy and somehow — he looked back on it

now and wondered how in the world they'd managed to pull it off — both made it out of college with teaching degrees. In the fifties! And black! Yeah, it was a miracle, a minor one, but life had all kinds of simple miracles if you'd just look around and notice them.

They'd gotten teaching jobs in their hometown, a tiny school district in Eastern Kentucky, one of only a handful of black people for a hundred miles in every direction. Of course, they only got the jobs because they were "local" and because the district didn't have a single white applicant. Nower County, Kentucky wasn't exactly a tour bus destination.

He taught math. She taught history. Life was good. Then Billy went off to Vietnam. Only eighteen years old! After two white soldiers in dress uniforms showed up on their porch one cold morning in January, there followed a decade of Cotton's life that was so dark he had trouble seeing into it in his memories.

But he had Thelma and together they made it through.

When the high school closed, Cotton couldn't find another teaching job so he took a job at a sewing machine factory and worked his way up to foreman. He liked the job. It was challenging, made him feel like he was earning his way in the world when the majority of the people in Nower County had rolled over on their backs, stuck their feet up in the air and surrendered. Took the government checks, did everything they could think of to beat the system and sank down into a place Cotton couldn't locate in his mind.

Thelma didn't get another teaching job, but they were fine on one paycheck. She indulged her hobby and her passion, genealogy and historical research, got so excited when she found the records on somebody's great-great-great grandfather you'd think she'd won the lottery. Met with her Bible study once a week, her sewing circle once a week, could quote Scripture like she'd been to seminary and made a mountain of quilts to donate to orphanages.

Cotton was a year away from retirement, fully vested in his pension and Social Security, and they'd do fine. He hadn't yet decided if he wanted to quit working, though. He enjoyed what he did and he was good at it — still, to kick back and go fishing every day had a certain appeal. In fact, he and Thelma had planned to spend Sunday afternoon looking at some brochures for "retirement homes" in Florida, just blue-sky dreaming.

But by Sunday afternoon, Thelma was gone. And the world — in all its particulars — reality that was the foundation of Cotton's existence had vanished in a puff of smoke.

Cotton pulled his car over to the curb and looked at the cardboard box the looters had left behind. And somehow, it seemed to symbolize the insanity of it all. A box full of wrenches and screwdrivers, hammers and bolt-cutters sitting all by itself on an empty sidewalk, in front of an empty store, in an empty county …

What should he do with the box? Go put it back in the store so the looters could come back later and get what they'd left behind? What was the point in that? Useless effort; why bother?

Yet he found he couldn't just drive away down the empty street past the empty stores and the dilapidated heaps, and leave the box sitting there. So, he got out, picked up the box and carried it back into the store. Lester'd outlined the tools on the store's walls in black Magic Marker, so it was easy for Cotton to see where the tools had been hanging. He put them back, one after the other until the box was empty, was tempted to sweep up the mess from the back door window the looters broke to get in. He didn't do that, though, just left the front door of the store standing wide open so the looters wouldn't have to go in through the back. Wouldn't want somebody to cut a finger on the broken glass.

Then he got into his car and drove south out of Persimmon Ridge with no particular destination in mind, just headed out toward the Middle of Nowhere.

Chapter Five

Stuart stepped up on the porch of the house at the base of Little Bear Mountain and knocked, listened for the patter of little feet. Merrie had decided when she was two years old that it was her job in life to go to the door to greet whoever it was who'd come to visit. Of course, she wasn't big enough to open the door, so she just stood in front of it, not unlike a puppy that needed to be let out to pee, and waited for someone bigger to do the honors.

There was no sound from inside.

He knocked again.

Then his heart kicked into a gallop and he knocked a third time, hard.

Still silence.

She wasn't home, that's all. Charlie and Merrie had gone somewhere. To the grocery store. Or the park. Did Nower County have a park? Of course she wasn't home — duh — the rental car wasn't in the driveway.

The rental she'd failed to return.

The one that was supposed to be back to the agency two weeks ago.

He opened the screen and knocked on the door itself.
Silence.

He turned and walked down the front steps and went around the house to the backyard. He opened the gate and noticed as he stepped into the yard that the door on the kiln sitting beside the garage had been taken off the hinges and now leaned against the side of it.

Stepping up onto the back porch, he knocked on the door, but really didn't expect anybody to come anymore. They weren't home but they'd be back and he'd just have to wait for them.

He reached down and tried the knob. The door wasn't locked. Charlie'd told him about that, how nobody in small towns locked their doors, but city-boy born and bred that he was, that seemed incomprehensible.

Opening the door a few inches, he called out.

"Charlie, are you home? Merrie?" And when he said the child's name, a lump formed in his throat and he had to swallow hard not to allow a sob to escape. He had concentrated on Charlie, only Charlie.

Charlie was missing and he had to find her.

It was Charlie who'd failed to return the rental and missed the calls to her publisher. Charlie.

But Merrie was *with* Charlie. Whatever had happened to Charlie had happened to precious little Merrie, too, and the thought of harm coming to that child filled him with a fear and dread he had not known existed in the world.

Merrie was Daddy's little girl. Charlie said he spoiled her, let her have her way, always gave in to what Charlie called her "drama queen" fake hysterics and he was aiding and abetting her tantrums.

To which he responded, *silently:* "Busted!"

He knew Charlie was right, of course. Made perfect sense. He'd trained dogs — okay, children were different in most respects but some fundamental principles applied. In both species, homo sapiens and canines, you did not reward unwanted behavior.

But Charlie being right, and Stuart knowing she was right, didn't change the fact that that little girl could look at him with those impossibly blue eyes and he would melt in a puddle and give her anything she wanted. He had promised Charlie dozens of times that he would be better about that, because he understood the tantrums that were cute at three would be nightmares at sixteen, but somehow he had not yet managed to get his behavior to line up with what it was proper to do.

He so desperately wanted to hear that chirpy little voice. He envisioned her opening her arms and squealing, "Daaa-deee!" and running to throw herself into his embrace, and the image was so powerful it took his breath away.

He opened the door the rest of the way and stepped into the kitchen, took only one step and stopped. Standing just inside the door of the empty kitchen instantly felt … intrusive somehow. Like he was … trespassing somewhere that he was not welcome. It also felt spooky in a way Stuart couldn't understand or explain. Creepy. How could a sunlit kitchen in a snug little house nestled up against a beautiful mountain feel … sinister? Absurd as it was, he sensed something threatening about it that made the hair on the back of his neck stand up and his heart take up the rhythm of a timpani drum.

It was crazy! But then, so was the guy who blew a hole in the road and then vanished without so much as the sparkle of a soap bubble.

He hadn't let himself think about that, hadn't let his mind go there because he didn't know what to do with it. Where did you put a thing like that? Either he'd imagined it — which he hadn't, there was, after all, a hole in the road to testify to what had happened — or he had been witness to something impossible. Both called his sanity into serious question.

And now he was standing here in a homey kitchen more afraid than he'd been as a little kid in a haunted house. Afraid of what?

The thing that didn't want him here.

The thought dropped into his mind out of nowhere, with the horrible ring of truth.

Something didn't want Stuart here. He was intruding into the realm of some powerful, malevolent force and that was a very dangerous thing to do.

"Nuts. That's nuts." He said the words out loud, in an effort to populate his out-of-control imagination with the normal and the ordinary. It didn't work. In fact — now he really did go to the end of the diving board and leap into the deep water — he could have sworn the words rode a puff of white out his mouth. Like on a winter morning.

How had it gotten cold in here?

Done! He'd have said that out loud, too, just like he had when he was standing in front of the hole the vanishing man had blown in the road. But he feared to speak, feared he'd see another puff of white.

Then he couldn't help calling, "Merrie! It's Daddy. Daddy's home."

And the words trailed out small clouds of white vapor and were greeted by silence. A loud silence that didn't sound hollow but should have because the kitchen was empty. Not just empty of people. There was a vacant space in front of the kitchen window where there should have been a table and chairs. He took a few more tentative steps into the room, far enough to see into the dining room, which had no table and chairs, either.

He resolutely crossed the kitchen, looking around in it for ... for what? For anything that would indicate Charlie had been here. The countertops were bare — no toaster or coffee pot or electric can opener. He reached out to open a cabinet, but drew his hand back, irrationally afraid that if he opened the door there'd be nothing inside and that would mean ...

A June calendar hung on the wall with a notation in Charlie's handwriting for a graveside service. Beside the calendar was an oversized kitchen blackboard with the title "Not in Kansas Anymore, *TO-DO*" and there was a lone to-do item written in the upper left corner: "get bird seed." Those words were *not* in Charlie's handwriting.

He crossed the dining room into the living room and froze. There were pictures on the walls — two little girls at various ages, Charlie and her older sister, Mallory. He just glanced at the photos, refused to allow his eyes to linger because the sight of Charlie as a gap-toothed first-grader hit him harder than any tackle ever had. There was a mirror beside a not-very-good oil painting of a vase and flowers. Nothing else. No furniture!

Charlie and Merrie couldn't have been *living* here!

Clearly, she had emptied the house out to prepare it for sale and she and Merrie were ... yeah, where? He wandered the rest of the house, his sense of unease growing with every breath, a desperate need to bolt out of the place without looking back held in check only with an enormous force of will.

All the floors were hardwood except in one bedroom. Thick carpet on the floor there showed the indentations of the bed, nightstands and a dresser. Deep indentations. He knelt and touched where one leg of a bed had been sitting. The carpet fibers were firmly crushed, packed tight, almost like the bed had been there only moments before. He picked at the dent with his fingers, and the fibers immediately began to let go, to straighten, to fill in the dent.

The absurdity struck him — who did he think he was, Tonto? *Three horses, Kimosabe, one with two riders, go north toward fort.*

He stood abruptly and strode back into the kitchen, forcing himself to move slowly and purposefully and not to give in to an absurd desire to go running out the door. The cold hit him like a fist. And the stuffiness was growing with every heartbeat, the sense that there was not enough air in the house. Or maybe that the room was — *too full,* somehow. Like it had too much in it, which made no sense at all since it was bare-bones empty.

He'd assumed in the beginning he would just wait here until Charlie got home from wherever she'd gone. Now … well, she would come back here eventually, even though she and Merrie were obviously staying somewhere else. He'd just have to leave her a note. He wanted her to know he'd been here, that he was trying to find her. Picking up a piece of chalk from the blackboard tray, he considered what to say, then just scribbled, like blurting out a word, the thought that was burning a brand in his mind.

"Where are you?"

He dropped the chalk back into the tray and stood looking at the words. What else? She needed to know that he would return, and keep coming back until—

Words appeared on the blackboard beneath what he had written. Just *appeared;* not there, then there. Charlie's handwriting.

I'm trapped. It won't let me go.

Stuart made some kind of sound, a mixture of a grunt, a sob, a cry and a scream, all of those and none of them. It was a distinctly man sound, like the sound the sidekick, never the hero, in childhood cowboy movies always made right before he looked down and saw the arrow in his chest.

He stared at the words, unable to process either the content of the message or its existence. Finally, he reached out slowly, his hands trembling, to touch them, but before his fingertips reached the blackboard, all the words began to vanish, his and the ones below. *As if they were being erased.* He stared in gap-jawed horror. In seconds, they were gone.

The words were as "not there" as the dude who'd blown a hole in the road right in the middle of the county line.

Stupidly looking around — *like maybe the words had dropped on the floor!* — took up the few seconds required for Stuart to process that what he had just written and the other words that appeared after it — *Charlie's response?* — had just *vanished.*

Then he was moving across the kitchen in great leaping strides, out the back door, and found himself sitting behind the wheel of the rented Lexus, breathing like he'd just returned a kickoff the full length of the field.

He started the engine, threw the car into reverse and pulled out of the driveway, turned and tore down Barber's Mill Road in the opposite direction from which he'd come … oh, not *toward* anything.

Just away. *Away.*

Chapter Six

Charlie McClintock started to reach for the cup of coffee Sam Sheridan had poured for her, then thought better of it. Her hands were still shaking like a jackhammer and she hadn't been able to take a few minutes sitting in her car outside the clinic to calm herself. Deputy Sheriff Liam Montgomery had come out the front door as soon as she pulled up.

"Don't suppose you've seen Reece Tibbits, have you?" he'd asked before he got into his cruiser, and she'd merely shaken her head, hadn't trusted her voice not to tremble. Gratefully, Merrie's cheerful babbling covered for her with Liam and with Raylynn when Charlie dropped the child off to assume her duties as the assistant-receptionist-in-charge-of-playing-with-the-puppies.

Neither Sam nor Malachi Tackett had picked up on how shaky Charlie was when she sat down at the break-room table, but they would if she spilled her coffee all over it! And then they'd ask what was wrong and Charlie did *not* want to talk about it. Couldn't talk about it, not until she

36

got her own arms around what had happened in her mother's kitchen this morning.

"So does this make us the Breakfast Club?" Sam asked.

Charlie and Malachi immediately got the reference to the movie and Malachi said, "Well, it is Saturday. And it feels like detention. None of us is here because we want to be."

They'd hastily arranged this morning's powwow because there were things they needed to talk about and they'd all been too fried last night, too traumatized by what Charlie and Malachi had encountered in Fearsome Hollow and by what'd happened to E.J. — mauled by a rabid dog!

Sam looked exhausted. She had spent the night looking after E.J. One of the things on the unwritten agenda for this morning was setting up a schedule for caring for E.J. Shifts. It would be no trouble to find volunteers to fill the slots and Sam couldn't do it all by herself.

"I am glad to assume the role of the bad boy," Malachi said. "I do not qualify for the nerd position and—"

"You're the jock!" Sam said. "Every girl in school sat in the stands drooling when you threw some Hail Mary pass right into Billy Joe Richland's hands."

Malachi looked both surprised and embarrassed. "Billy Joe was the one catching the ball. That's the hard part. And then he had to manage not to get tackled. I just mailed the package and stood there while he delivered it."

"I want to be Molly Ringwald," Charlie said in a voice that was almost normal, barely any tremor in it at all. She was gradually getting her mojo back.

"Well, duh," Sam said. "There wasn't a girl jock and I'm not the girl with hair in her face … what was her name?"

"Actually, we're all the nerd," Malachi said. "At least we were our senior year. In English class at least."

"I still don't understand why the whole class wasn't as captured by *The Lord of the Rings* as we were," Sam said.

"As Mama has so often pointed out to me, 'ugly's on your face, but stupid goes all the way to the bone,'" Malachi said. "I don't think the rest of the class wanted to believe in magic."

"Well, they believe in it *now*, whether they want to or not," Sam said.

"Is that it — magic?" Charlie asked. "Do you think that's what's going on here?"

Was what Charlie had seen in her mother's kitchen this morning magic?

CHARLIE SITS *on the kitchen floor, not because she decided to sit but because her legs folded up and dumped her there.*

She stares at the blackboard on the wall and screams "Nooooo!" at the top of her lungs. Except she doesn't. She screams it in her head because the wind has been so totally knocked out of her she doesn't have the breath to scream.

She shakes her head, squeezes her eyes tight shut and then peeks out at the world through a forest of eyelashes. Reality refuses to budge.

So she opens her eyes wide and stares in gap-jawed amazement at the words in the center of the blackboard.

Not the words her mother had written, words Charlie could not, would not erase. Not "get bird seed" in her mother's precise cursive in the top left corner.

Other words, big and bold — three of them.

Where are you?

She recognizes the handwriting. It's Stuart's.

She grinds her teeth together. Stuart wants to know where she is? Riiiiight. Like he cares where she is!

Leaping to her feet, she rushes to the blackboard, picks up the piece of chalk and writes beneath the three words.

"I'm trapped. It won't let me go!"

She stares at what she wrote, wondering why her mind had burped out those particular words. She starts to write more, describe that she's right here where Stuart had left her *when he sneaked off to Hawaii with* ... somebody ... *instead of going to a business meeting in Seattle. She looks at the chalkboard through a blur of tears.*

Grabbing the eraser out of the tray, she applies it with force to the blackboard. Careful not to erase "get bird seed," she wipes out everything else, wipes over and over until every speck of chalk is gone.

NO, there was nothing magical about the words on the blackboard in Charlie's mother's kitchen. Charlie had written them herself — that was the only possible explanation. She had gone home last night so distraught she didn't even remember doing it. The words were nothing more than her own pathetic effort to make it seem like Stuart gave a rip what happened to her and Merrie. The man had made it abundantly clear that he did not!

"I guess that's what we're here to talk about," Sam said. "What it is — the Jabberwock."

"And what to do about it," Charlie said. "That's the point."

"But those are sequential questions," Malachi said. "You can't link the progression to the second without figuring out the first."

Malachi continued to surprise Charlie. That wasn't what you expected to hear from a man who'd grown up without a telephone, falling asleep every night with the heady aroma of the privy outside in his nostrils.

He had always been a conundrum, even when she wouldn't have known the definition of that word. He'd come back to Nowhere County from ... Rwanda, she thought ... broken, shattered by horrors they couldn't imagine, but there was strength in his determination to hang on. She glanced at Sam and saw a brief look of admiration wash across her face, gone almost before it formed.

"Our mission, should we choose to accept it, is …" Sam ran out of steam. "Is what?"

"To save E.J.'s life," Malachi said softly. And then it was quiet.

"If he doesn't get a rabies vaccination before he starts to develop symptoms …" Sam said.

"We have — worst case scenario, one week to figure this out or E.J. dies of rabies," Malachi said.

"And even aside from that, he's not doing very well," Sam said.

"What do you mean?" Charlie asked.

"He's running a low-grade fever. And I don't know why. Or what to do about it, except tell him to take two aspirins and call me in the morning. He needs to be in a hospital — a human one — and he needs a doctor. Several doctors."

"Several?" Charlie repeated.

"A vascular surgeon, for starters. I'm concerned about blood flow down the injured leg — it was so … damaged. "

"Whether it's rabies or merely complications of being mauled by a dog, it all loops back to the same thing," Malachi said.

"The Jabberwock." They said the word almost in unison, and it creeped Charlie out.

"As far as I can tell, nobody else is thinking long term. Everybody just assumes it will go away as mysteriously as it arrived and they're focused on surviving until it does."

"And it could," Sam said.

"It won't," Malachi said, and Charlie didn't like the finality in his voice.

40

"You keep saying things like that, as if you know something the rest of us don't. You want to share it?" Sam asked.

Malachi was silent, looking at his hands. Then he lifted his eyes and looked from one to the other of them.

"We need to get our heads out of the sand. This thing isn't a naturally occurring phenomenon, some atmospheric anomaly brought on by the storm the night before. Whatever it is, it's … outside nature."

"Are you saying it's … supernatural?"

"You can tag it with that term if you need a hook to hang it on. All I know is that it has a will and it has superimposed itself on nature, has taken over control of aspects of the natural functioning of the universe. In more ways than just a mirage and Star Trek transporter."

"Abner's house," Charlie said simply.

"And the mist. A shame you missed that little joyride," Malachi told Sam. "Besides being a barrel of fun, our little adventure gave us some vital information."

"And that is …?"

"We may not know *what* the Jabberwock is, but now we do know *where* it is. It's in the mist in Fearsome Hollow."

Chapter Seven

Cotton Jackson slowed as he approached four-way stop at the intersection of Route 17 with County Road 278, where the Dollar General Store and a bus shelter were on his left beneath a sign that said the Middle of Nowhere. He didn't intend to stop. Nobody stopped there; slowed down maybe, but didn't stop. You weren't likely to get t-boned because you could see down the cross road for half a mile in both directions.

What Cotton saw barreling down County Road 278 was a red car, maybe a Lexus. He stopped then, sat there. The speed that vehicle was traveling, there was no way for it to stop at the sign, even though it was clear Cotton was waiting to cross the intersection.

Cotton was certain the car would blow through the sign and keep going. But it didn't. It appeared that as soon as the driver noticed Cotton, he began to try to stop — a process that didn't succeed in halting the car until it was well past the sign and thirty feet down the road beyond it.

The backup lights turned on, but the car didn't back up the way it'd come. The back end swung around, pointing the car toward where Cotton was stopped at the sign. Then the car — it was, indeed, a Lexus — slowly approached until the driver's window was next to his.

The man driving it was a black man, but at that moment he looked ghostly pale, and only another black man would notice the difference. The window powered down. Cotton's was already down. The man started to speak and couldn't seem to form words. He looked really familiar, but Cotton couldn't place him.

"You're the first person I've seen since I got here. There's not another car on the road, no people. It's like … like everybody in the whole county vanished."

"They did."

Cotton watched reactions wash across the man's face. Shock. Disbelief. Horror. And then a kind of relief. When he spoke again, there was more life in his words.

"Where'd they go?"

"I got no idea."

The man took a second to absorb that, then said, "My name's Stuart McClintock and—"

That's where Cotton had seen the guy's face! Of course. Cotton Jackson was a diehard Pittsburgh Steelers fan! He could quote every one of Stuart McClintock's stats: grew up on the streets of Detroit, recruited from some inner-city high school by every Division One college football program east of the Mississippi River. Legendary running back for the University of Michigan. Heisman Trophy winner his senior year. First-round draft pick by the Pittsburg Steelers. McClintock had had a bright future before a career-ending knee injury during his third season sent him out to "get on with his life's work," as Coach Chuck Noll put it, instead of to the Super Bowl. Cotton thought he'd heard McClintock went to law school.

"—you don't know me, but—"

"Oh, I know you, alright. I bleed black and gold!"

The man offered the scraps of a smile before he continued. "Look, I'd like to talk, to ask ... I was wondering if—"

Cotton was sure he didn't usually have so much trouble putting words together. But then, discovering that everything you thought you knew about the functioning of the universe didn't mean diddly squat would rattle anybody.

"Can we go somewhere? I'd like to buy you a cup of coffee—"

"There's nowhere to go for coffee. Nobody here to serve it."

Even that small statement rocked McClintock and Cotton realized he wasn't displaying a whole lot of sympathy and empathy for this stranger — famous football player that he was — who was just finding out what had knocked Cotton on his keister almost two weeks ago.

"Why don't you follow me to my house. I live on Chimney Rock Pike in Bugtussle Hollow. It's not far. Not a whole lot there, but I did get a table and a couple of chairs to go with my camping gear out of the U-Store-It. And a coffee pot. I'll make you a cup. Of course, by the time I'm finished talking, you're going to need something a whole lot more potent than coffee. A stiff drink. Strong enough to dissolve the swizzle stick."

An hour and two full pots of coffee later, Cotton sat back and surveyed the young man seated across the table from him. Stuart McClintock had told Cotton an outrageous, impossible story, one Cotton was certain the man would never have breathed a word about to anybody else on the planet. Knew the breakers would fire in McClintock's head at how "crazy" he sounded and he'd tell himself it hadn't really happened, loud enough and long enough to mostly convince himself that it hadn't. Mostly.

But there'd been no disbelief on Cotton's face when he began his halting account, and as Cotton merely nodded, he spoke more and more freely. The explosion. The vanishing man. The cold. The appearing/disappearing words.

"Her mother's house was bone *empty* — not a stick of furniture in it — so how could she have been living there?" Then he'd looked around but hadn't yet asked Cotton why he had so little furniture. But he had wanted to know if Cotton would mind if he opened a window, though, that the room was "stuffy" — so he felt that part, too.

Well, now it was Cotton's turn.

Chapter Eight

Malachi was right, of course. Whatever the Jabberwock was, it "lived" in Fearsome Hollow. Charlie remembered the mist and almost shuddered. The Jabberwock was hidden in that mist. Or maybe the Jabberwock *was* the mist.

"This isn't just about Abner's house, and all the other houses that have aged a hundred years overnight," Sam said. "It's about *Abner*. Where is he?"

"We could look under every rock in Nowhere County and not find him," Malachi said. "He's not here anymore."

"Then where is he?" Sam's voice was close to a strangled sob.

"The witch warned us," Charlie said. "When she gave us the rocks, she said that when she got back to Gideon after spending the night in the woods, her family's house was bare — all the houses were — no furniture, no food, no possessions, nothing in them, but—"

"—her family was still *there*, still in Gideon ... somewhere," Sam finished for her.

"*For a while*," Malachi said. "Her father left the rocks

for her for three days. Maybe from inside Gideon looking out there was a mirage around it, like out there on the county line. Remember when Liam tossed those rocks on J-Day, how they bounced right through it to the other side? I bet that's what the witch's father was doing — throwing rocks through a mirage."

"*For three days*, but after that it 'took them' — whatever 'took them' means," Sam said.

Charlie knew what it meant. So did Sam, whose voice was huskier than usual when she answered her own question. "It means 'vanished.' Like Abner."

Charlie had a sudden, crazy thought. She knew it had grown out of what had happened in her kitchen this morning — what she *thought* had happened — but she voiced it anyway. "You don't suppose that ... there are people in Nowhere County right now who came looking for somebody and found ... nothing but empty houses — all the people vanished?"

"We have bigger fish to fry than wasting time wondering what people *outside* the Jabberwock are doing," Malachi said. "If the Jabberwock 'took' the people in Gideon, and Abner, then by logical progression it will—"

"Take all of us eventually just like it took them," Sam completed his thought.

"Only there are a whole lot more of us," Charlie said. "Nowhere County's way bigger than Gideon."

"You think it took the sky then, too?" Sam said.

"The sky?"

"Well, the stars anyway."

"You've been talking to Pete," Malachi said and Sam nodded. "The stars in the night sky. They're ... wrong. And the uniformity. Weather, temperature. It's artificial."

Charlie knew without asking what he was talking about, had wondered about it herself — no clouds, and

47

every morning it was sixty-five degrees when she got up and eighty at noon. Every day. But she had blown it off. Malachi didn't miss much.

"And time," Sam said.

"You think so, too, huh?" Malachi noticed Charlie's confusion, that she wasn't privy to the understanding that had passed between him and Sam. "It's not something definitive, something you can quantify. It's not like looking at a sky without constellations and the stars don't twinkle, or temperature as predictable as a thermostat. But time is passing … *too fast*. And it's getting faster every day."

"Too fast …?"

"It doesn't take a whole hour for an hour to pass. And the clocks are synced to … Jabberwock time … so you don't notice."

"Then how *do* you know?"

"I've spent weeks, months of my life an hour at a time walking guard duty. Your body learns to measure, knows when your replacement will arrive. Now it's off somehow, all wrong. Minutes, hours … maybe even days are passing here faster than they are" — he made an all-encompassing gesture that indicated the rest of the known universe — "out there."

"It's definitive." Sam's voice was soft. "Rusty has an hourglass. It came with a chemistry set, I think. I don't remember. He brought it to me a couple of days ago and said he'd watched the sand drain out of one glass into the other and it was off, wrong. So we sat, watched it together. When the clock on the wall said an hour had passed, there was still sand in the glass. Another sixteen minutes' worth."

Charlie felt an awful chill settle into her bones.

"Abner's house had … *aged*," she said. "The Jabberwock controls … *time*?"

"Not just Abner's house," Malachi said. "I've seen others."

"I have, too." Sam and Malachi traveled the back roads into the mountains and had seen what Charlie hadn't.

"If the Jabberwock is not just a phenomenon but a being with a will, then it has a purpose. There's a reason it's here." Malachi sounded like he knew what that reason was, or thought he did.

"What is it?" Charlie asked. "What's the reason?"

Malachi didn't say anything, then dodged the question altogether with, "Maybe somebody at tonight's meeting knows."

That was something else they needed to talk about — the meeting Deputy Sheriff Liam Montgomery had coaxed the county's founder, Sebastian Nower, into setting up tonight.

"We're going to have to dump on everybody else tonight what we suspect," Charlie said, looked at the other two and amended, "what we have *figured out* — that people are vanishing. Maybe if everybody in the whole county puts their heads together, we could—"

"You get to deliver the bad news," Sam said to Malachi. "Less likely somebody will decide to shoot the messenger if it's you."

There was a sudden commotion outside the door and Roscoe Tungate rushed in without knocking. His eyes were wild, his voice trembled.

"Harry's gone!"

"Gone?" Charlie knew she sounded like a parrot. She also knew what he meant without having to ask and the knowing of it made her sick to her stomach.

"Gone! You got to help me find him, please. *Pleeease*, help me."

He sounded like he was about to cry.

"I knew it when it happened. Me'n Harry ... we're connected. We're ... it's a thing, we know if there's something bad ... I *felt it* when it hit Harry. The cold! And he hollered, 'No!' And now I can't ... get through to him. I ain't never had to *try* to communicate with Harry. It was just there, you know. But I been trying and ... I hear that sound, not loud, but I hear it. That ... *static*."

"Have you gone to his house to try to find him?" Sam asked.

"No. I come here first." Tears began to run down his cheeks.

Roscoe lived on Burnt Stump Road on the south side of Callahan Mountain and Harry lived in Solomon Hollow on the north side. The Middle of Nowhere was the opposite direction, but Roscoe'd come here *first*. Clearly, he was afraid of what he would find at Harry's and didn't want to go alone.

"I'll help you look for him," Malachi said, getting to his feet.

Roscoe nodded, relieved, but didn't say anything. Maybe he couldn't. He just turned and strode purposefully out of the room.

Malachi spoke quietly, maybe just to himself. "Picking us off, one by one. And eventually ..."

Charlie thought of Gideon, looked from Sam to Malachi, and fear passed among them as real as the chill Charlie'd felt *breathing* out of Abner's front door.

"I'll be back in time for the meeting," Malachi told her and Sam, and then he was gone.

Chapter Nine

After the Breakfast Club adjourned — Malachi to go with Roscoe Tungate to look for Harry and Charlie to take Merrie home for a nap so she wouldn't be grumpy at tonight's meeting — all the air drained out of Sam. She felt flat, used up. She needed to go home. Both Judd Perkins and his daughter, Doreen, were caring for E.J. now — well, watching him sleep, anyway. Doreen had surprisingly good first aid skills, had taken a class from the fire department. And Judd ... on some basic human level his hulking presence — useless though he might be — was a comfort. Besides, he refused to leave, had sent his daughter and granddaughters home last night after cameo appearances to thank E.J. for saving the children's lives from the rabid Great Pyrenees that had mauled him. Doreen had returned early this morning, but Judd had remained stalwartly present through the night. Buster had, after all, been Judd's dog and E.J. had gone out to the Perkins' farm because Judd had called to report that Buster was "acting funny."

Sam sighed. Judd might be harder to get rid of than a

bad cold, but that was a concern for another time. Right now, Sam was focused on only one thing — going home and spending time with Rusty. She was neglecting the boy, had been ever since J-Day. Had been so busy, with so much to do to care for the Nower County residents trapped by the Jabberwock who were turning to her and E.J. now as the only available sources of medical care.

She absolutely should not have that responsibility. Sam was *not* qualified, *not* trained, but she'd done things in the past week she would lose her LPN license for if the Kentucky Board of Medical Licensure found out about it.

She didn't think they would find out, though, and she leapt away from that thought and all that it implied like she'd touched her tongue to hot coffee.

During her training, Sam had worked in the trauma center of the University of Kentucky Medical Center and had waded through gunshot wounds, amputated toes, splinters through the leg and a kid who had somehow gotten a fishhook caught in his jaw.

She had "participated in" the treatment of those — meaning she had observed, watched, helped. Was the person who handed the attending physician the hemostat, or bandaged the wound after the emergency room doctor had sewn up the gash.

But Sam had only *watched*.

In the past week, *she'd* been the one using the hemostat to control bleeding on wounds she absolutely should not have attempted to repair. Like E.J.'s. But if she didn't, who would?

There hadn't been a huge number of cases. It wasn't like in a county this size folks were always swallowing AAA batteries — the toddler who'd shown up in the emergency room at UKMC after he did that had died. But whatever it was that happened, stubbed toe or dog mauling, she was it.

Now that E.J. was out of commission, she was literally the only medical care there was. The buck stopped at Martha Ann Sheridan, aka Sam, Licensed Practical Nurse, and if she screwed it up there wasn't anybody to come along behind her and fix it.

Everybody in the county needed her. But so did her twelve-hear-old son! Oh, sure, you'd have to pull his fingernails out to get him to admit it, but Rusty needed his mother's comfort right now. The world had turned totally upside down. Life as we know it on the planet had taken a hike and Rusty was putting a brave face on it, being a man about it. On the outside. She knew if she scratched very deep she would find a scared little boy.

Sam was determined to go home and spend all afternoon scratching.

But before she could get out the door, Raylynn came to tell her someone was in the waiting room to see her. Raylynn had been instructed to schedule appointments — unless the patient was bleeding or having chest pains, something life threatening — but Raylynn said the girl in the waiting room had refused to go home.

Sitting slumped in a chair by the door was Hayley Norman, dressed fashionably in grunge — army boots with laces untied that looked like small cars on her feet, cargo pants, and a flannel shirt over a shapeless tee-shirt intentionally splotched with stains on the faded brown surface. Her hair was a bird-nest tangle. It was not a flattering look for a girl at least a hundred pounds overweight but style had trumped flattering. Hayley leapt up as soon as she spotted Sam and rushed toward her, obviously armed with arguments and rebuttals to keep from being put off again.

"I know you're busy and I get that, but I don't need but

a couple of minutes of your time and I have to talk to you, I really do. *I have to*."

The girl spewed it out in one long speech, punctuated by the hiccupping breathing that accompanied a little kid's crying jag. Or a grownup's desperation.

Taking Hayley by the hand, Sam lead her to a chair and sat down. Hayley was surprised, had likely expected much more resistance than this. It was like shoving as hard as you can on a locked door, and when it's unlocked you stumble through, off balance.

"What can I help you with, Hayley?"

Hayley looked around, like there might be somebody lurking in a dark corner, eagerly eavesdropping on their conversation. The room was empty.

Still, she asked, "Could we go somewhere … you know, private? What I need to talk about is personal and—"

"There's nobody here." Sam's voice sounded as tired as she felt. "Moving into another empty room where there's also nobody there won't be any more private."

Hayley sat, reluctantly.

"I don't mean to be abrupt, but it's been a really long day, and with E.J. …."

"Yeah, I heard everybody talking about how he got bit by a dog that had rabies. But E.J.'s not going to get it, is he? I mean, you can give him something, a shot or something, and he'll be fine — right? He's a really nice man, a kind man." Hayley paused for a beat, her eyes unfocused. "He's a 'for real,' like you."

"For real?"

"A for-real good person. Not just pretending so he can get bonus points for being nice to the fat girl."

Sam was surprised by that. Most sixteen-year-olds she knew were … well, sixteen. Crass. Self-centered, self-absorbed. Certainly not as self-aware as Hayley, who also didn't appear to be bitter or entitled, and didn't hide behind the chirpy-happy facade that many morbidly obese people used to cover the self-loathing pain that ate at their souls. Hayley Norman was unexpectedly "real" and Sam admired her.

"E.J. will be fine. Now, please tell me how I can help you."

"Well …" She took a deep breath and spouted what Sam could see was a released speech.

"I know it's probably not something you normally do, but drastic times call for drastic measures, right? This is an emergency, being stuck here unable to get out, and in an emergency all bets are off. I know—"

"Get to the point, Hayley. What do you want?"

"An abortion."

Sam shouldn't have been surprised, but she was. Oh, not that the girl was pregnant. She would gladly stand up before the High Court of Community Standards and Societal Condemnation and testify that it happened — even to "good girls." What surprised her was the brazen request.

Could I have an abortion, please, and would you supersize my fries?

Sam managed to keep her voice level and professional when she replied.

"I don't do abortions."

"Of course you don't. I mean, normally you don't, but you can make an exception in an emergency and this is an emergency. This is a matter of life and death."

"Is there something wrong — with you? Or the baby? Did your doctor—?"

"Oh, I haven't been to a doctor! I couldn't do *that*, sit in the waiting room and everybody wondering what you're doing there because you don't look sick."

"If you haven't been to a doctor, how do you know—?"

"I went to a drug store in Lexington when I went up there for the Community Church's Youth Congress and got a pregnancy test. The little line turned red."

"Those aren't always accurate—"

"And then I went to Planned Parenthood and got an examination. They set me up with a doctor to do the abort … the procedure."

Planned Parenthood. Not Sam Sheridan's favorite organization. A far better title would be Planned Abortions — you get knocked up, we get you un-knocked-up. They guided all the girls who flowed through their doors, scared teenagers who didn't know jack, into the willing hands of the abortion mills that scraped the babies out of their bellies and told them everything would be fine, it was just tissue, after all, not a life, a real human, a *baby*.

"And it's just, you know, it's not like it's a real … person or anything like that. It's just a bunch of cells, tissue." Hayley sounded like a parrot. "Because if it was a b—" Her eyes filled instantly with tears and a blink sent them cascading down her round cheeks. "But it's *not*. They said it wasn't. And so did Sugar Bear. It's just a … a … it's not a …"

It would have been cruel for Sam to point out that an abortion wouldn't make Hayley un-pregnant, it would just make her the mother of a dead baby. It was clear Hayley already knew that part. She just wasn't quite ready to face it yet.

"Hayley, I don't want there to be any mistaking what I am about to say. Listen up. I do *not* do abortions." When Hayley started to interrupt, Sam raised her hand for silence and continued. "Not now. Not ever. Not in an 'emergency'—"

"You don't understand. I can't be pregnant. My father is a *minister*."

Who is about to be a grandfather. That's what Sam wanted to say, but didn't. Hayley wasn't finished.

"And Sugar Bear ... he gave me the money to pay for the abortion. I was on my way there when I hit the Jabberwock."

"Sugar Bear?"

"That's what he told me to call him. It's a secret that we're seeing each other."

Translate that: he's a married man.

"He gave me the money and then I didn't get it. He told me to get you to do it and if you don't ..."

"You better figure out something to say to 'Sugar Bear,' Hayley. I won't perform an abortion." She had to hold up her hand again. "This isn't a debate, Hayley. The answer is a forever, unequivocal *no.*"

Sam got to her feet. Hayley sat where she was.

"I'm sorry." Sam turned toward the door.

"What's going to happen to me?" Hayley said, not in a dramatic *what'll-I-doooo?* sort of way. Sam could hear the pain and fear in her voice and was moved to compassion.

She turned back to the girl and said as kindly as she could. "What's going to happen is you're going to have a baby. A *baby!*" She reached down and patted the teenager's hand reassuringly. "These things have a way of working out for the best. Really. You'll see."

Chapter Ten

Nower County, Kentucky Deputy Sheriff Liam Montgomery found Reece Tibbits's truck just where Lonnie Monroe'd said it'd be. Lonnie'd got up early to work in the garden he'd decided he'd better plant in his backyard. Farmer's Almanac said not to plant seeds in the heat of the day so he'd got up before dawn. Lonnie was a laid-off coal miner collecting black lung benefits whose knowledge of horticulture did not extend past mowing his grass when it needed it, snipping off the fuzzy heads of the crop of dandelions that called his yard home and wondering sometimes why there always seemed to be more and more of the little critters.

He'd heard an explosion. Wasn't a miner anywhere who didn't recognize that sound. It had come from Lexington Road about half a mile away. Lonnie was curious, but he had to get the planting part right or the seeds wouldn't never turn into nothing and he was coming around to the belief that it'd be a real good thing to grow food for yourself — what with the Jabberwock and all.

When he'd finally checked on the origin of the sound, he'd called Liam.

"There's a big hole in the road, right in the middle," he'd said. "When I went out to have a look-see, wasn't nobody there, so I dug around in the glove box of the truck. Papers say it belongs to Reece Tibbits. There was a rifle laying there in the road, a 30.06, good-looking deer rifle, just laying there. It must belong to Reece, too. Whenever you find him, you tell him I'm keeping it for him."

Reece Tibbits had a bit of a reputation as a brawler. He was big and strong; Lonnie Monroe was neither, so he wanted to stay on Reece's good side.

"Must have left his truck there and decided to ride the Jabberwock to the Middle of Nowhere."

That was ridiculous. Nobody, well, not anybody with a lick of sense, voluntarily "rode the Jabberwock" anymore. Not after that first day when nobody knew what it was and folks went wandering off into it on their way out of the county, or heard about it and came down to the Middle of Nowhere to see the casualties. Nobody, not even a stupid teenager, would get anywhere near the Jabberwock now, not after what'd happened to Abby Clayton. How she exploded.

Liam had checked with Sam anyway before he drove out here and she'd said she hadn't seen Reece.

Pulling up behind the truck, Liam got out of the county's lone remaining cruiser, the one the sheriff had left parked behind the sheriff's office when he went off on his fishing trip two days before J-Day. He left the bubble light flashing, not that anybody was likely to come barreling down the road and rear-end him. Wasn't any reason for anybody to come down the road at all, given that it dead-ended right here, closed by the Jabberwock.

So what was Reece Tibbits doing here?

Liam examined the truck. The tailgate was down, so Reece had unloaded something out of the truck bed. Wasn't hard to guess what that'd been, given the gigantic hole in the road right beneath the Jabberwock. Reece'd come out here with some kind explosive device, determined to blow a hole in the Jabberwock. Liam got it — Reece's mother was dying because she couldn't get her dialysis treatments in Carlisle and folks said Reece was losing it.

So where was Reece now? Obviously, his attempt to blast out of the Jabberwock had been unsuccessful. It was still there, shimmering across the road. Liam approached it carefully, the way you'd get close to a cobra in a basket with some dude doing his flute trick to get the snake to rise up out of it. Truth was, he couldn't get close to the Jabberwock without climbing down into the hole Reece had blasted in the asphalt directly under it.

Liam stood looking at the shimmer. At his own reflection in the shimmer. At how the shimmer didn't reflect Reece's truck or Liam's cruiser behind it, only reflected the sky and clouds … and people. Nothing else.

The keys weren't in the truck or Liam would have started it and pulled it off onto the shoulder of the road. He checked the fuel gauge — three quarters of a tank. Somebody would come along — likely Lonnie Monroe as soon as Liam left — and siphon that gas out.

Liam got back in his cruiser and made a U-turn in the middle of the road and headed down Lexington Road toward Sugar Bowl Mountain. Reece Tibbits lived outside Bennetville on Cicada Springs Road. Since he'd already checked the Middle of Nowhere and Reece wasn't there puking his guts up, where was he? And what was Liam going to do when he found him? Arrest him for blowing a hole in the road? It was, after all, against the law to do a thing like that. But folks were doing a lot of things now that were against the law and Liam couldn't arrest them all. Or even some of them. What would he do with a prisoner in the county's tiny jail?

Liam had no idea, had been puzzling over that and the implications of law enforcement in general ever since he'd gone chasing after the speeder with Pennsylvania plates and found himself with a needle inside his skull in the bus shelter in the Middle of Nowhere.

Did he have the authority to arrest people? Now, given … well, everything? Arrest who? People were committing "crimes" all over the place, stealing the gas out of the cars of their neighbors who'd been out of town on J-Day. And stealing whatever else they fancied that was property belonging to people who were as stuck out there as he and all the other nowhere people were stuck in here.

If he didn't enforce all the laws, how did he decide which ones were really crimes, given the present circumstances? Everybody knew Viola Tackett had stationed her boys at Foodtown — to prevent hoarding, or so she'd said. Liam had no doubt that Viola Tackett, civic-minded citizen that she'd always been, was merely guarding the contents of the store for herself. The only weapon she'd used was intimidation, veiled threats. So did he go out past Killarney to the Tackett household on Gizzard Ridge and arrest the lot of them for terroristic threatening? Not likely.

Who did he arrest, then? The people looting the few remaining downtown businesses in the Ridge? Most of them did it in broad daylight, didn't bother to wait until dark when most of the streetlights didn't work. How long would it be before the whole county went dark? Yeah, the electricity was generated in Drayton County by the Rural Electric Coop Corp and was on a grid — he didn't understand that part — that served a six-county area that included Nower County. So there'd be electricity here until … what happened when the people here stopped paying their electric bills? Surely the RECC would notice eventually and cut off service.

People stayed clear of the businesses whose owners were still here, though. Mostly. But somebody — teenagers, perhaps — had broken into Lester Peetree's hardware store, vandalized the place and took all the guns and ammunition. Candy and soft drinks, too. What did teenagers plan to do with the weaponry — if it had, indeed, been teenagers who took it? Should Liam be out there trying to find out? And what if somebody got so desperate for a rocking chair or a footstool or a lampshade that they showed up at Stovall's Used Furniture Store with a gun and demanded that Joe Stovall hand one over? There probably weren't half a dozen people in the whole county who didn't have access to some kind of firearm. So what if somebody used a weapon to steal something? Armed robbery wasn't a crime you could let slide.

Liam probably hadn't slept more than a couple of hours a night since J-Day. Not so much stewing over what was happening, but worried sick about what he was supposed to do about it. Then he'd let it go and accepted that he'd just have to figure it out as he went along. One thing at a time. That was the best Liam could do until the county meeting tonight. He had invested a lot of emotional capital in the meeting and desperately wanted to believe that something would come of it.

Figuring folks might not show up if "the law" called a meeting, Liam convinced Sebastian Nower to call it. The great-great grandson of the county's founder was a bombastic blowhard who loved nothing more than the sound of his own voice. If he got the upper hand, he'd do all the talking, fight to the death to make sure things were done whatever way he wanted them done, and then preen around importantly, finally given the respect due him for his stellar genetics and lineage.

Liam couldn't let that happen.

It had taken two weeks' worth of soul searching for Liam to come around to an understanding of the new nature of the universe and his own place in it. He believed dire circumstances made great men. There was lots of historic proof of that — like Alvin York, that World War I soldier from a farm in Tennessee who killed all those Germans, or that Texas soldier, Audie Murphy, who became a movie star. Men who stepped forward when the need arose and made a difference. Liam Montgomery was determined to be that man in Nower County. *Somebody* had to step into the leadership vacuum that existed here, somebody willing to make the hard calls and suffer the consequences of his decisions. He believed the county's 3,500 residents were teetering on the brink of chaos. And he genuinely believed that was the county population, no matter what Viola Tackett said, though, granted, they certainly hadn't all been inside the county's borders when the Jabberwock locked the doors. Out of all those people, Liam Montgomery was the only person who could lay claim to *legitimate authority*.

He would man up when the time came, take charge.

Oh, it wasn't like Liam was looking forward to what lay ahead, but he could clearly see his duty and he would perform it to his dying breath. He wasn't looking forward to questioning Reece Tibbits, either, didn't have any idea what he'd do with the man once he had. The only thing he was certain of was that the doing of it was *his* responsibility. If Liam didn't take charge, who would?

Chapter Eleven

The old black man seated across the table from Stuart hadn't lost even half a step in his mental fitness, was sharp, articulate — a bit stiff and unyielding, but that was to be expected, given that he'd never met Stuart. And Stuart tried to keep reminding himself that he was ... what was it Charlie had called it? Oh yeah, Stuart was from "Away from Here," which made him and everything he said suspect. But Cotton Jackson didn't strike Stuart as that clannish. Maybe he was just reserved because the subject matter called for reserve. For skepticism. Should be taken with a dump-truck load of salt.

Stuart McClintock had never spoken nor listened to anything as lock-me-up-with-the-rest-of-the-looney-tunes-in-Saint-Somebody's-Home-for-the-Bewildered-and-swallow-the-key as what was said in that kitchen that day.

The kitchen was in a tidy brick house with a manicured yard and rose bushes growing in rich profusion around the porch. When Stuart leaned over to smell one of the blossoms, Cotton said merely, "Thelma," and there was such longing in the single word it broke Stuart's heart.

The kitchen that was almost bare — a table, chairs, coffee pot, and four cups in an otherwise empty cabinet. There was no furniture in the dining room or den, which Stuart could see from the kitchen, just bare hardwood floors, not even so much as a throw rug.

It looked just like Charlie's mother's house had looked.

There were pictures on the walls, though, and even from where he stood in the kitchen, Stuart could tell that the shots were of a family of three — mother, father and a little boy — who grew up in other pictures into a handsome man in a uniform. The standard "soldier" picture hung above the mantle, blown up huge, with medals arranged beside it in the frame. It had the look of a memorial, so Stuart didn't ask.

Stuart took off his suit jacket and draped it over the back of the chair, unbuttoned his shirtsleeves and rolled them up to his elbows while Cotton made coffee. After he'd served Stuart the promised cup — Stuart took it with cream and sugar but was reluctant to ask because he suspected Cotton didn't have any of either — Cotton began the conversation by answering a question Stuart hadn't asked.

"Because I was my parents' eleventh child and my father's response to finding out my mother was pregnant with me was, 'I don't *cotton* to having another mouth to feed.'"

Then the old man described coming home on Sunday afternoon, June 4, exhausted from a short night of sleep, looking forward to a hot meal and a soft bed. He'd tried several times to call and tell his wife what time to expect him, but she didn't answer. Which was odd, but he let it go.

"I felt something … strange when I pulled into the driveway. I felt … frightened. And that was crazy, but I couldn't help it. I felt … afraid."

Stuart thought about how he'd felt earlier sitting in the driveway of Charlie's mother's house.

"Her car wasn't in the driveway, but I figured she'd just put it into the garage. Thelma wasn't home. Wasn't … anywhere. And the house was *bare* … nothing in it, no furniture, clothes, dishes, duct tape, pillow cases, drain cleaner … *nothing.* Absolutely nothing."

He was so horrified and mystified and terrified that he …

"Ran around like a chicken with my head cut off."

He thoroughly searched the premises for Thelma — the house, the yard, the garage, the little patch of garden behind the garage, the attic and basement, and started trying to call family members, neighbors … anybody. Nobody answered. The phones just rang and rang. Obviously there was something wrong with the lines, some kind of outage.

So he got back into his car and went looking for Thelma.

And discovered that not only was Thelma missing, so was everybody else in the county. He went to house after house and found them all empty — furniture and belongings gone, no cars in the driveways, nobody home.

When he'd completed his story, Stuart blurted out the first thing that came to his mind — "that's the craziest tale I ever heard" — and immediately regretted being blunt and rude.

Cotton didn't seem to be offended, just stood, took Stuart's coffee cup and turned to the sink where there were already a couple of dirty plates and some silverware.

"We got a dishwasher." He nodded toward the appliance under the countertop. "Wanna know how spoiled I am? I never learned how to run the thing, so …"

He gestured toward the sink.

"I went to Walmart in Carlisle for what I absolutely had to have" — nodded toward the card table and folding chairs — "thought I got everything, but forgot to get a dish drainer."

Rinsing the cup and spoon, he set them in the sink beside the other dishes, then turned toward the door.

"The man you described, the guy who blew a hole in the road and then went poof and vanished—" Stuart winced at the reference, but it was indeed what he had said. Actually, the man had done a two-fer, had appeared out of nowhere and then disappeared into nowhere. "I know a man named Reece Tibbits, who had to be the guy you saw. He lives on Sugar Bowl Mountain off Cicada Springs Road with his wife, Cissy, and daughters — Sue-Sue and … Patty, I think. How about we go pay them a visit?"

Cotton drove. In an era when everybody else in the world was ditching their gas-guzzlers for Hondas and Toyotas, Cotton Jackson drove a 1993 Chrysler Concorde. Big and roomy. As they wound around through the mountains, Stuart would have been hopelessly lost if Cotton hadn't provided a running-commentary geography lesson.

Chimney Rock Pike to Elkhorn Road to CR 278 W, then onto Barber's Mill Road, the road where Charlie's mother's house was located, only they turned south on it instead of north. That led to Gallagher Station Road and they turned right on it onto Cicada Springs Road.

Cotton stopped at every house they passed. Went to the door and knocked. Called out, looked in the yard and in the outbuildings.

Nothing.

Nobody.

One after another.

When they pulled into the driveway of an old house

that was literally falling down, the roof had collapsed on the back and the chimney had fallen over into the yard, Cotton just sat, looking at it.

"This is Reece Tibbits's place," he said.

Stuart must have misunderstood what Cotton'd told him because he'd thought they were going to the place the Tibbits guy and his family *lived,* not some house maybe his grandparents grew up in. Stuart started to ask questions, but Cotton's face silenced him. The man looked not only troubled, but enlightened, a guy who had just solved a mystery, had figured out where the next lightning bolt was going to strike — but realized he was standing on the spot.

Though he was convinced by the parade of empty houses that the whole population of the county had … well, at least they were not there, Stuart wasn't ready yet to own "vanished."

Cotton didn't stop anymore at every house they passed as they left the "weathered estate" of the Reece Tibbits family and drove back through the Middle of Nowhere where he'd met Cotton and on into an actual small town Cotton said had once been "incorporated," though Stuart didn't know what that meant. The name of the town was Persimmon Ridge. It was a ghost town. No one on the street. The stores closed. Not boarded up, just closed. Like somebody would come back in after their lunch break and open them for business. Stuart rubbernecked at all the emptiness, his grip on what he considered "reality" growing looser by the second.

They passed a store with a sign that identified it as Peetree's Hardware Store and Cotton pulled up in front of it and stopped briefly.

"Front door's closed," he said. "No cut fingers."

Stuart was by this time so stunned, had had the breath

so totally knocked out of him that he didn't even ask what Cotton was talking about.

They hadn't stopped at the handful of houses they'd passed on the way to Persimmon Ridge that were just as old as the Tibbits place, relics nobody'd lived in for years, generations. Cotton had identified them as they passed, though. "That's the Johnson place," he had said of a pile of rotted timber that hadn't been a habitable abode in half a century. Or simply, "The Pruitts."

When they passed a couple of businesses in Persimmon Ridge that were in the same condition as the Tibbits's "estate," Stuart was curious, found it hard to fathom how the businesses in the small town that might not look thriving but were still at least *serviceable*, could be shoulder to shoulder on the street with dilapidated relics. Why hadn't the town or the nearby business owners gotten rid of the shacks?

When he asked, Cotton gave him a look that Stuart was beginning to interpret as: "You ready for this?" He wasn't, but pushed forward.

"Why have they been left standing?"

"Because this time yesterday, or last week or Arbor Day, they weren't relics. They looked just like the buildings around them. They weren't ... *old*."

Now *that* was insanity.

"They weren't old? How does a building suddenly get ... old? And why?"

"I don't have any idea, but I'm developing a theory. You seeing Reece out there this morning, vanishing out of the middle of the road, got me thinking." He pulled into an empty parking space beside a whole street full of empty parking spaces and turned to look at Stuart. "I drove past Reece Tibbits's house yesterday." He said the words slowly, reluctantly. "It was ... just your basic little three-bedroom clapboard house. Paint was beginning to peel but not bad. Grass needed mowing. It was just like all the others we've passed today … nobody was home. But now …"

Stuart suddenly understood.

"Are you telling me that falling-down shack on Cicada Springs Road was Reece Tibbits's home? I thought you'd taken me to see where his grandmother was born or something."

"Yesterday it was … just a house. Today it's … aged a century. And Reece *vanished* this morning. I'm wondering … what's the connection?"

Stuart was still a step behind, trying to wrap his mind around it, that the falling-down ruin he'd seen a little while ago had been a normal house twenty-four hours ago, a place somebody lived. Except, well, nobody did.

He couldn't see any connection, but he let it go, let it all go, no longer able to contain the biggest question of all, the one that'd been buzzing around in his head since he met Cotton.

"Why didn't you tell anybody about this, Cotton? Why didn't you report it to the police? A whole county full of people — how many is that?" Cotton just shrugged, his mind clearly somewhere else. "Okay, a thousand people, let's say it's a thousand people, *two* thousand — and they're gone. Why didn't you call the authorities?"

Cotton gave him a look that was almost sad, like he knew what he was about to say was not going to received well.

"I did report it, Stuart. To every state agency I could find and tried to get the federal government involved."

"And …?"

"And nothing. They didn't do a thing."

"Why not?"

Stuart's mind was spinning.

Cotton said nothing, then held up his finger, the way you do to say, "Wait, I have just one more thing."

"But before I show you, I want you to do something for me, okay?"

"Okay."

Cotton reached past Stuart and dug around in the glove box of his car, and pulled out a piece of paper — actually, it was the envelope to use to mail in your fine for a parking ticket — and a pen. He handed the paper to Stuart.

Stuart thought about what he'd written on the chalkboard in Charlie's kitchen, what had happened next, and clenched his teeth, bulging out the muscle in his jaw.

Cotton saw it.

"This will be like that. It will totally creep you out. But a picture is worth a thousand words, saves a lot of explaining." He handed him the pen. "Write a note to yourself. Put down the time and the date and then jot down — just a couple of sentences — what you've seen in the past couple of hours."

"But why—?"

"Just do it. Humor me."

Stuart took the paper and pen and jotted down the empty houses, the old shacks, and the man who disappeared after he blew a hole in the road. It was hard to make himself put down the part about the note to Charlie that had vanished but he forced himself to do it.

He held out the paper to Cotton, who held up his hand and shook his head.

"It's not for me. It's for you. I want you to put that in your shirt pocket."

"What are we doing here?"

"Just do it! I don't have the energy to argue with you."

Stuart folded the paper and slipped it into his shirt pocket.

Cotton started the car and pulled out of the parking place.

"Where are we going now?"

"To my house to get your car so you can drive us to Carlisle, the county seat of Beaufort County." Cotton paused. "Well, at least part of the way there."

Chapter Twelve

Liam was on his way from Reece Tibbits's house to talk to Reece's mother, Grace. And how was he going to tell her what he'd found at Reece's place? The woman was dying! How could he tell her that something totally impossible had happened? She wouldn't believe him, he didn't think, and then he'd have to take her there and show her. He was not looking forward to that.

What was happening?

Of course, that was the essential question about everything in life these days. *What was happening?*

How could Reece Tibbits's house have … have aged, turned into a dilapidated pile of rotting timber when yesterday it had been …

Where was Cissy? Reece's wife was a quiet woman. Liam wouldn't use the word mousey but everybody else did. And in truth it fit. She was small, unassuming, with her shoulders hunched most of the time and her eyes averted. He had never heard her say more than two or three words at a stretch, though he understood from Reece's drinking buddies that he complained about her incessant whining, nagging him to do first one thing and then another until he retreated to his woodshop, the only place he could go to be free of her because she was allergic to sawdust.

Where was *she*?

And the girls? Reece had two daughters, teenagers, as quiet and unassuming as their mother. Where were Sue-Sue and Patty?

"Unit two, this is dispatch, come back," came the words out of his radio. Seriously. Unit two? There were no units one or three or four or … he was the *only* unit, but Betty Greenleaf was … best described as the star of her own movie.

"This is Unit two."

"Unit two … we have a reported code ten, eight, seven at 1235 Sugarloaf Lane in the Ridge." Her voice was hushed. From the gravity of the situation, of course. Unless she'd gotten her codes wrong — which she hadn't because they hung on a chart right in front of the radio unit and she'd pronounced each number separately like she'd been trained to — then she was dispatching him to a murder scene. The tingle of excitement he heard underlying her words convinced him she hadn't screwed up the codes, didn't think she was telling him about a dog off the leash instead of a dead body.

"A 10-87 on Sugarloaf Lane. Copy."

Grace Tibbits would have to wait.

When he rolled into the driveway of Martha Whittiker's house you'd have thought the circus had come to town. Must have been a dozen people, all excited, being held back behind a makeshift police line by Homer Pettigrew, a volunteer fireman.

"Boy, am I glad to see you, Liam." Homer handed the end of the piece of extension cord he'd stretched from

Mrs. Whittiker's back porch railing to the little cottage in her backyard. "It's all yours."

With that, Homer turned his back and walked away.

Liam looked around frantically, trying to find somebody responsible.

Not in this crowd. Her neighbors, mostly. Elderly people who had congregated in her yard like vultures about to pick at roadkill.

Somebody had to … he spotted Holmes Fischer at the edge of the crowd.

"Fish!" he cried.

Fish looked for a moment like he wanted to turn tail and run. He didn't, just nodded, tried to hang a half smile on his face that fell totally off one side.

"Yeah, Liam. What can I—?"

"Come over here and take the end of this line," Liam said, motioning with his hand. "Come on, hurry up." Fish didn't move any faster. Liam handed him the end of the extension cord. "Hold this. We're all pretending this is an official police line, like the ones with the little yellow flags with the words "police line" written on them. This is all we got. You hold this and don't let anybody through."

Fish looked like he wanted to throw up, but he took the piece of extension cord as it occurred to Liam that it was a sad state of affairs when the most reliable person in a crowd of a dozen people was a homeless drunk.

"Okay, listen up, everybody," Liam called out to the crowd. "I want you all to stay back, don't get any closer—"

"They said she got her head all bashed in," Roberta McCreedy said. "Like smashed her face. Zat true, Liam?"

He ignored her but Wilbur Berg didn't. "I seen her body. I was the one called, Liam. She got whacked on the head alright, but didn't bash it in. But she's dead. Not no doubt about that. I thought she might be unconscious, then I touched her. Cold as a popsicle."

"Musta fell down, huh, Wilbur?" Ethel Porter said.

"She didn't fall down. Somebody cracked her on the skull!"

"We got a killer on the loose?" Wilma Thacker had a voice like a rooster. "Is that what you're sayin'? A *murderer*?"

"No, I ain't saying—"

"I don't even lock my doors and there's a *killer* out there!" Ethel Porter squeaked out the words in a half-scream. "Preys on old ladies! Oh, dear Jesus."

"Will you all be quiet!" Liam shouted. And he was proud of how stern and official he sounded. "We don't know how Martha Whittiker died." He shot Wilbur Berg a look. "If she is, indeed, deceased. Let's show a little respect for Mrs. Whittiker and not be running off at the mouth about her when you have absolutely *no* information."

That shut them up. It would until he was out of sight, but that was the best he could do. He walked down the little stone path to the door of the cottage where Martha Whittiker allowed her druggie grandson to live. Word had it Dylan wasn't just an addict but a dealer. Liam didn't know that to be fact, but most rumors had a least a kernel of truth in them and Liam figured this one had a whole ear of corn. All of which begged the question: what possible motive could the boy have to harm his grandmother — biting the hand that feeds you and all that?

Wilbur Berg had dipped under the extension cord Liam had given to Fish and followed Liam to the door, babbling as he came.

"… asked me three days ago did I want her chest freezer and of course I said yes. Seen her car in the driveway so I knew she was home but when I knocked on her door she didn't answer and I found her laying right where she is now."

Liam was about to ask how Wilbur'd seen the woman on the floor in the cottage when the curtains on the windows were drawn tight shut, but Wilbur answered before he had a chance.

"Oh, I went looking everywhere — her car being in the driveway and all. Searched her house but she wasn't nowhere, so I come here next."

"The door to the cottage was closed, but you opened it?"

"Sure I opened it. How else could I have got inside?"

Wilbur likely saw the disapproval on Liam's face.

"But I didn't touch nothing, didn't 'contaminate the crime scene.' I watch *Hill Street Blues*."

Well, at least he hadn't—

"You ain't supposed to move the body of somebody's been murdered because you might mess up something." Wilbur paused, then continued proudly. "So I didn't do *nothing*."

Liam had time for one breath.

"Except, you know, cover her up, of course. Couldn't just leave her laying there like that! So I took the afghan off the couch, rolled her over and laid it down, then rolled her back and covered her. Got blood on my shoe but I wiped it off. Wasn't hardly no blood at all but I'm squeamish so I came outside then and vomited."

Liam felt like vomiting, too.

Still, Wilbur hadn't dragged the team of Clydesdales and the Budweiser beer wagon through the place, so there was that.

"Looked to me like there was blood on the front door, but I knew better than to touch it. I watch all them cop shows."

Liam glanced at the front door and saw smudges that could possibly have been blood.

On the *outside* of the door.

If she was murdered in the cottage, the killer might have gotten her blood on his hands and smeared it on the door when he left. But he would have smeared it on the *inside* of the door, not the outside. Only way there'd be blood on the outside of the door was if somebody had it on their hands going in.

Chapter Thirteen

Stuart McClintock didn't have anything to say as he piloted his rented red Lexus away from Cotton's house, following directions toward the county line. But the former football star was going to have plenty to say when they got back! Cotton felt a wave of pity for the man whose world Cotton was about to rock to the core.

Just like Cotton's had been rocked two weeks ago.

He told Stuart the story, gave him the CliffsNotes, anyway. The whole story was ... even now it was hard to think about.

COTTON JACKSON STANDS *in his sister-in-law's living room in the little community of Twig* — her *bare living room* — *and shouts at the top of his lungs, "Ophelia, where are you?"*

His voice is tear-clotted, doesn't even sound like his own, and he can feel tears running down his face but he isn't aware of crying. He has just come from the Greenleaf place, had raced down Chimney Rock Pike to his nearest neighbors. Betty Greenleaf is the dispatcher at the sheriff's department, Arnie raises pigs. The pigs were there; Arnie and Betty and their sad-eyed little basset hound weren't. After that he had backtracked, turned off on Elkhorn Road and stopped at the Potters' and the Throckmortons'. Nobody was home. Becky Sue Potter is pregnant, due any day now. Sweet little Sarah Throckmorton, who looks like Tweety Bird's grandmother, was gone — along with everything she owned. Including a whole herd of cats.

All the houses were empty. Bare. Not a stick of furniture, nothing left but the pictures on the walls.

More important than the missing furniture was the missing people.

There was nobody, not anywhere.

Everybody was gone.

"You answer me, do you hear? Stop this foolishness and answer me — Ophelia."

Silence, a dark, heavy silence.

That's when he loses it, his control on his emotions, allows himself to topple off the edge into hysteria. Panic.

He isn't aware of running out to his car, of turning around and driving so fast down County Road 278 East that it's a good thing there is no traffic because he would have run them off into a ditch.

No traffic. No traffic! He blows through the Middle of Nowhere — not a car in the Dollar General Store parking lot. Empty.

The nearest Kentucky State Police Post is #7 in Richmond. It is a forty-five-minute drive away and he could have called. But Cotton has to tell another live human being. Not make some report over the phone, but look a man in the eye and say that he needed help, that his wife was missing, that everybody in the whole county was missing with her.

He remembers little of the drive to Richmond. The post is on Eastern Bypass, not far from the campus of Eastern Kentucky University.

He leaps out of his car. Leaves his door open, can't hold onto his terror and panic a second longer and bursts into the outer office huff-

ing, puffing and sobbing, crying out to anybody who'll listen. "They're gone. All of them. Everybody's gone."

A gray uniformed officer is suddenly at his side, taking his arm, and it feels more like restraint than compassion so he tries to shake free.

"You got to help me, you got to come look, come see. They're gone."

The officer doesn't release his grip. He's a white man and Cotton's rational mind, which has long since given over control of his behavior, notes the disdain in his voice that translates easily: Why should I believe a black man? Though he's not thinking "black," but Cotton will not allow himself even to think the n-word.

"Why don't you sit down right over in here?" and he's ushered by two officers, both white, into a small room with a table and Cotton wants to scream. It looks for all the world like every interrogation room in every cop show he ever saw. There's no mirror on the wall, but there is a video camera in the corner. And only a table and straight-backed chairs. He knows he has to get a grip on his emotions, that he sounds like a lunatic, but he knows if he can just get them to listen, get them to come and see, he won't seem like a lunatic anymore.

"Now what is your name, sir?"

"I'm Cotton Jackson and—"

"Where do you live, Mr. Jackson?"

"In Nower County," he says, then shouts, can't help it. "That's where I just came from, Nower County, and nobody's there. Everybody's vanished."

Shouldn't have used the word vanished. Gone was acceptable. Missing, even. But vanished definitely slammed doors in their minds.

"What do you mean vanished?"

"How many things can vanished mean? Gone. Not there. Nobody in the county is there."

"Sir, are you telling me—?"

He grabs hold of his emotions and with the greatest amount of restraint he has ever displayed in his whole life, he says, "Don't listen to me. Don't believe a word I say. Write me off as a raving lunatic … just come see for yourself. You see for yourself and you won't have to question my sanity."

One of the officers leaves and the other takes down Cotton's story, which is so disjointed he wouldn't have believed a word of it if somebody had told it to him.

The first officer returns with two more officers, one older, clearly the man in charge.

"I have raised Unit 17, Trooper Jim Burton. He's in Beaufort County right now working a wreck, and he will get there as soon as—"

"Have I broken any laws?

It is such a non sequitur none of the officers answer.

"Because if I haven't and you're not putting me under arrest, then I respectfully request to be allowed to leave."

"And go where?"

"To the FBI in Lexington. Somebody somewhere has got to listen to me and take me seriously."

The three officers exchange a look.

"You are not in any emotional condition to drive a car right now, Mr. Jackson and—" says the officer with the blond hair, the first one, whose gold name tag on the black pocket flap of his gray uniform identifies him as Trooper J.R. Barker.

Cotton interrupts. *"So you're saying I can't leave?"*

"I am saying that you can't drive," says the guy in charge, Captain Tomlinson. He is a black man. Maybe that will help. *"I am going to dispatch these two officers to go back home with you and investigate your claims."*

Cotton looked up at the ceiling with tears in his eyes, *"Thank you Jesus,"* he said.

He rides in the back seat of the sleek gray cruiser with Trooper Tomlinson. Trooper M.L. McMichael follows, in Cotton's Chrysler. As they drive, Cotton tries to explain, as best he can, what he has seen. He has calmed down some, sounds a little less homicidal, and he *can tell that the officer is at least interested. Oh, it's clear he doesn't believe a thing Cotton is saying, but he is at least listening.*

As soon as they cross the county line from Beaufort into Nower County, Cotton directs the officer to pull over at the first house they pass.

"Why stop here? Who are these people?"

"I don't know who lives here, officer. I just know they're not here. And there's no furniture in their house either. I'll wait here. You go see for yourself."

The other officer pulls in behind and the two of them go up the sidewalk to the door and knock, try to raise somebody, look around the property. Cotton hears Trooper Tomlinson tell Trooper McMichael, "There's no car here. They're just not home."

Cotton calls out from the back seat of the cruiser.

"Let's try the next house, then."

And they do. They stop at the Donaldson house — Burt's an older man who has a young wife and a house full of little kids. But the kid paraphernalia that ought to be all over the yard — bikes and trikes and Big Wheels — is gone.

He waits in the car as the two officers go to the door. He can't hear what they're saying as they walk around, trying to find the Donaldsons — knocking on the back door, checking out the garage and the backyard. They don't go inside the house because the doors are locked and they don't have a search warrant.

Cotton can tell they're still not buying what he's selling.

They almost pass the next house, but Cotton directs them to stop. It's the house belonging to Bobby Joe Mattingly, and it is a falling-down wreck.

"Surely nobody lives here," said Trooper McMichael.

Cotton opens his mouth to tell them that yes, indeed somebody lives here, or did when he drove past the place on his way to work Saturday morning. The Mattinglys. The house had been a complete dump then, your basic Appalachian poor man's shack complete with the requisite dead-car lawn art. But it didn't look a hundred years old like it does now.

"Look, can we go to my house now, please," Cotton begs. The officers confer, and then Trooper Tomlinson returns to his cruiser and directs Cotton to get out of the back seat and into his own car, that Trooper McMichael had been driving. Tomlinson gets behind the wheel.

"You direct me to your house while Trooper McMichael does some looking around, finds some neighbors who might be able to tell us what happened."

"There aren't any neighbors to tell you what happened because whatever it is, it happened to them, too."

But Cotton sees the disbelief and slumps back in the seat.

"You'll see. Let your buddy go looking. You'll see."

The remainder of the afternoon begins to telescope, like Cotton's at one end of a dark tunnel, the nightmare dream of running toward a light that remains uniformly out in front of you.

Trooper Tomlinson looks around Cotton's bare house without comment, just goes out to sit on the porch and wait for his partner. McMichael shows up at Cotton's house an hour later, tells Tomlinson that he could find nobody. That he went into the town of Persimmon Ridge, a little unincorporated wide-spot-in-the-road, and no one was there, either.

"Houses that weren't locked, I went inside. Four of them. They were all … empty. Bare. No furniture. Nothing."

Cotton can see the officers are spooked. Good. They need to be spooked. Spooked is the absolutely appropriate response to what is happening.

Trooper McMichael must have radioed the state police post because a third Kentucky State Police patrol car rolls up in Cotton's driveway. The officer in it confers with the other officers.

"Mr. Jackson," says Trooper Tomlinson, "we're going to do some more investigating but I'll have to ask you to remain here." He held up the keys to Cotton's Chrysler. "I'll return these when we come back."

So Cotton stays home, so emotionally wrung out now he is incapable of hysteria. He sits on his porch, trying to figure out what the officers will do, who they will call, what other agencies they will get involved. The three of them have been taking notes on little jot-down pads, to enter into some kind of official reports when they get back to the post, he supposed.

How do you fill out a missing person's report on a whole county?

By late afternoon, the three officers are again congregated in Cotton's driveway beside the two patrol vehicles. They're no longer skeptical, no longer believe he is a candidate for the Kentucky Home for the Bewildered. They get it now. They believe. Clearly, they don't understand any more about what's going on than he does, but they are all, finally, singing from the same sheet of music.

"We need to talk to the captain — all three of us together," *Trooper Tomlinson says, and Cotton doesn't have to ask why. "It's up to him what happens next." Tomlinson has become a human being since he first ushered Cotton into the back of his cruiser hours ago. Not just a human being — a scared one.*

"We'll make our reports, and ..." His voice trails off. "And then I don't know what will happen. I've ... we've never seen anything like—"

He lets it go, tells Cotton to expect their return as well as the arrival of who knows what other resources, agencies, what not. Shoot, maybe they'll send in the National Guard — how much manpower do you need to look for a whole county full of people?

Though by now, Cotton doesn't think the people are ... somewhere, all being held captive by ... He has come around to the belief that what happened to them happened all at once to all of them. And there are no explanations of what that could possibly be that don't involve aliens or psychic phenomena or ... he doesn't know what.

The troopers get in their vehicles and drive away.

And they never come back.

Chapter Fourteen

After Sam Sheridan told Hayley she would not perform an abortion, Hayley went out to her car and bawled. Correction — her father's car. The Jabberwock had eaten her mother's car and that had caused a kerfuffle of major proportions.

She'd come up with the only lie she could think of at the time. Not very plausible or believable, but the available evidence was inarguable. She'd just decided to go for a drive, she'd said, wanted to get out of the house, didn't look where she was going, didn't intend to leave the county but … bada boom, bada bing, the Jabberwock.

She hadn't been able to track Sam Sheridan down and ask for her help until now because she'd been grounded, not allowed to go anywhere *for two weeks.* Everybody in the whole county was already grounded, so that made Hayley doubled-grounded.

How other families were dealing with the incredible impossibility that wrecked all their lives was a mystery to Hayley. She only knew what was going on at her house. Her mother cried almost all the time, and her father had retreated into a sulking, angry silence — a reaction she had never seen in him. She thought she understood. It wasn't like the Jabberwock was a character out of the Old Testament. One of the prophets, maybe — Nehemiah, Jeremiah, Jabberwock, Isaiah ... something like that. Or maybe Jesus had met the Jabberwock beside the Sea of Galilee, and she had missed that part altogether. Truth was, her father was beside himself because he could not fit the reality of the world out there with what he knew about God. Did God cause it? At the very least, he had allowed it. And her father's beseeching prayers to the contrary, God wasn't heeding requests to get rid of it, either.

She genuinely pitied her father. How did a man like that fit it all into his head?

Maybe everybody was responding like her father — sulking and angry. She wouldn't know. She had nobody to ask. She didn't have any friends. Oh, there were a handful of other teenagers in the youth groups in her father's various little congregations who'd have *claimed* Hayley as their friend because being friendly to the fat girl was the Christian thing to do. But they weren't real friends. When she'd stared gap-jawed at the red line on the pregnancy test indicator, had burst so suddenly and abruptly into tears that she caused a nosebleed, she didn't have a soul to confide in. Not one girlfriend to call who would commiserate, empathize. In fact, the girls she knew would be genuinely surprised Hayley had gotten pregnant at all because, well, a certain behavior was required to initiate that particular physical outcome, and who'd want to do *that* with Hayley Norman?

Hayley sat in the parking lot of the Dollar General Store, where she'd parked so nobody would see the car at the veterinary clinic that people knew had been transformed into a people clinic. If somebody saw her car there and told her father, what would she do?

Now that seemed like a pitiful consideration, cast into shadow by the bigger reality that Sam Sheridan would not help. Sam had said no, she wouldn't get rid of the baby—

Hayley stopped breathing. Froze in place like an ice sculpture.

The baby.

She'd never said that before, never thought that thought before. Maybe it was because Sam refused to call the abortion "getting rid of tissue."

No, that wasn't why. She'd called it a baby for another reason that had been growing inside her as surely as the … the baby. The realization that she was carrying a baby, a human being. A little girl or a little boy that was much more than a mass of tissues to be scraped out of her uterus. Hayley had somebody's life in her hands, and it looked like she wasn't going to be able to … to kill it.

She was so staggered by her own thoughts it was like somebody had slapped her in the face. *Kill it?* Like getting an abortion was killing something. No, some*one*.

But it was. And once the blinders of abject terror fell off Hayley's eyes she knew that, had known it all along but wouldn't admit it.

She had come to it, the end of all things, sitting in the parking lot of the Dollar General Store that still smelled, would likely always smell, just a little like puke.

No more options. She couldn't get an abortion. Which meant that she couldn't get un-pregnant.

She would have to … have the baby.

Waves of terror-nausea washed over her.

She would have to tell her parents. Her father. Admit that she had …

He would ground her for the rest of her life. At that

thought she bleated out a burst of laughter that wasn't appropriate to her current circumstances and yet ...

Ground her for the rest of her life? She was *pregnant*, was going to have a baby. Not being allowed to go to the movies — which she couldn't now anyway — or out riding around with friends — who had never really wanted her along with them in the first place — seemed a paltry punishment.

But one other implication of "grounded for the rest of her life" that she now had to consider was the fact that if she couldn't leave the house, she couldn't see Sugar Bear.

Sugar Bear.

He'd wanted her to get an abortion because that was the only way they could keep seeing each other.

Not only would she have to tell her father, she would have to tell Sugar Bear. He had responded with something like terror when she'd told him she was pregnant. He'd almost seemed more afraid than she was. When he'd recovered his composure, he'd told her that he was afraid he'd never be able to see her again and he couldn't stand that thought. He'd said she had to get an abortion, offered no other alternative. Now that she couldn't ... what would he do?

And when her father demanded to know who was the father of the baby, as he surely would do, what could she say? She couldn't admit it was ... Sugar Bear. The nuclear explosion that would cause would lay waste to her whole family ... and Sugar Bear's. It was absolutely unthinkable. She would simply have to refuse to identify the father.

Refuse.

Hayley had never, not once in her sixteen years, displayed outright defiance to her father's wishes. She had done all manner of things he had told her not to do, of course, not the least of which was having sex! But she had never looked the man in the eye and refused to do what he wanted.

How could she ...?

How could she tell Sugar Bear, and she would have to tell him *before* she told her parents. Once she told her parents, her life as she had known it was over. She would never have another chance to see Sugar Bear.

Yeah, with her rolls of belly fat beneath a wardrobe of oversized tee-shirts for disguise, it would be easier for her to hide a pregnancy than for girls like Megan Callison, who reminded Hayley of the scrawny chickens Megan's mother'd been hauling in the back of her pickup when she rode the Jabberwock on J-Day. Or skinny-minny Chastity Manning, whose father owned Foodtown. *Chastity.* Right. She was a backseat *warrior* — had flat-backed there with every boy in a three-county area. But eventually, there would be no hiding Hayley's pregnancy and if her father figured it out before she had a chance to tell him ...

She'd call Sugar Bear as soon as she got home. She could meet him tonight because her parents were going to some kind of county meeting at West Liberty Middle School in the Ridge and wouldn't be home. Since the Jabberwock, he was a lot easier to reach, no longer feared that his wife might answer the phone when Hayley called. He had told her the day he had given her the envelope full of money that his wife was suspicious, had been "snooping around" — whatever that meant — was asking questions, putting him on the spot. But his wife had been out of town on J-Day, so she was no longer a problem.

Sugar Bear had to be first. Then her parents. She'd call Sugar Bear as soon as she got home and tell him they had to talk — tonight while her parents were at that county meeting. When her parents got home from the meeting, she'd tell them.

Tell them what?

She sat very still.

And what would she say to Sugar Bear?

A totally new thought began to form, tiny … like maybe *just a few cells.*

She'd tell him the truth. Reality. She'd tell him she was going to have a baby … and she intended to keep it.

Chapter Fifteen

"Never came back?" Stuart was incredulous. "How … what …?"

"Boggles the mind, doesn't it?" Cotton pointed out the back side of the Welcome to NoWherE County sign coming up on their right and directed Stuart to pull over on the side of the road. "Stuart, you are about to find out why they didn't come back."

Cotton gestured down the road leading into Beaufort County. "There's a little convenience store about two miles from here. I want you to drive us there. I'm not going to say anything else. Just drive there and stop, and then … everything will make sense."

Stuart doubted seriously that there was any sense to be made of any of it, but he did as he was instructed because he didn't know what else to do. He pulled the red Lexus back onto the road and kept driving.

The Jiffy Shop where Stuart pulled in a few minutes later had propane gas canisters for sale on one side of the front door and bagged ice from a machine for sale on the other. A man came out of the store as Stuart pulled up. Bib overalls, filthy tee-shirt underneath, jaw swollen by a plug of tobacco, barefoot. Barefoot! Surely he and the guy who blew a hole in the road had been extras in the same movie — *Deliverance*. A sign advertising that Kentucky Lottery tickets were for sale inside proclaimed, "Somebody's got to win. Might as well be you."

Stuart felt a little strange, almost like he'd just awakened after a nap, thoughts jumbled, wasn't sure why he'd stopped — he was thirsty. Yeah, that was it. He'd stopped for a soft drink.

When Stuart came out of the Jiffy Shop with a soft drink, he found an older black man leaning up against the hood of the Lexus. He had no change to give the man and certainly didn't have time for panhandlers right now. He had to find some other route into Nower County because the road from Lexington had a hole in it the size of a Sherman Tank. And the man who blew the hole ... no, *not* going there.

"Stuart," the man said.

"How do you know my name?" Stuart asked. And as he examined the old man closer he realized that he didn't look like a panhandler. But how did he know Stuart's name?

"I'm Cotton Jackson," the man said, but didn't extend his hand as if he were introducing himself.

"What can I do for you, Mr. Jackson?"

The man pointed to Stuart's shirt pocket. "You can take that piece of paper out of your pocket and read it."

"What piece of—"

When he patted his pocket there was, indeed, a piece of paper in it. How'd this guy ...? Stuart was instantly suspicious.

"Look, I don't know who you are or what you want, but—"

"Mr. McClintock, you are looking for your wife and your little girl so you're in a hurry." Stuart's shock must have shown on his face.

"How—?"

"Just read what's on the paper," the man said. "Read it … and then we'll talk."

Stuart took the piece of paper out of his pocket. There were words written on the back of it — a DMV envelop to use for a mail-in parking fine. He looked at the words. They were in his own handwriting, but they made no sense.

"All the houses are empty. There's nobody here, everyone has vanished," the first sentence said.

Stuart's head snapped up and he looked in shocked surprise at the old man, whose expression hadn't changed.

"I wrote words on a blackboard and then other words appeared beneath them. Then all the words vanished."

Stuart was so shocked he couldn't speak. How … why …?

"Mr. McClintock, if you'd just give me a ride …" He pointed in the direction the woman at the register said was Nower County. "It's not but a couple of miles and you're going that way anyway. Do that, and I'll explain how we met each other."

Stuart was suspicious, wary of getting in the car with this man who obviously was a couple of sandwiches shy of a full picnic. But he didn't look … dangerous.

"I'm not armed," the man said, as if he'd read Stuart's mind. He lifted his jacket out to show pockets, turned so Stuart could see he had nothing concealed down the back of his pants. "You're a great big football player and I'm a wimpy old man. What harm can it do?"

Stuart was consumed with curiosity, and totally confused, so he gestured to the passenger side door.

"Get in. It'll be interesting to hear what you have to say."

"You have no idea how interesting."

A few minutes later, Stuart pointed at the Welcome to Nower County sign just up ahead.

"My wife told me about that, how teenagers added the H and the E and nobody changed it because it seemed to fit."

"*Charlie* told you," the man said as they passed the sign.

"Yeah, Charlie. How do you know …?"

And then Stuart knew.

It was all there, everything that had been … gone.

What in the world …?

He was suddenly terrified, as terrified as he'd been when the Tibbits guy blew up the road. And then vanished. As terrified as he'd been in Charlie's kitchen watching words disappear off a blackboard – his words and hers, too. They *were* her words! Weren't they?

"You best pull over, son," Cotton said, and he could see from the concern on the man's face that he had registered Stuart's emotional state.

Stuart managed to pilot the car onto the shoulder of the road. Then he leapt out of it, put his hands on his knees and vomited violently into the dirt. The nausea had hammered him without warning, a horrifying clenching in his gut that wouldn't let up until he had emptied out all the contents. And even then, he continued to reflexively dry-heave.

When it was finally over, he staggered back against the car, gasping for breath.

"You might feel better if you get back in and close the door," Cotton said from the front seat. "Smelling that won't do anything for your stomach and it's sure not doing anything for mine."

Stuart got into the car, closed the door, put the car in gear and drove fifty or sixty feet before stopping again. Then sat for a few minutes, panting.

"You knew this would happen. That was what the note was about."

"I didn't know that this *specifically* would happen, that you'd even forget who I was, that you'd get sick, but I knew something like it would, pieced it together."

"That's why …"

"Why nobody did anything about what's going on here. No sense bothering you with all the other places I went, things I tried. And not just me. I've run into other folks, a dozen or more people who came home to nothing like I did. People who did the same thing I did – they went to the police. Simple mountain people, uneducated – I'm probably the most credible of the lot. The same thing happened to them. I've even met two other people who showed up here later, like you did; one was a guy looking for his grandmother. It always ends the same. It stays here, in Nower County. Whatever you saw or did inside the borders of Nower County -- it doesn't leave with you. You forget all about it."

"That's impossible!"

Cotton lifted his eyebrows. "You sure about that?"

"This isn't real. This cannot be happening." Stuart's mind went into full bore revolt. "Things like this don't happen in the world. Vanishing people, vanishing belongings—"

"Vanishing memories. The constant in all of it is 'vanishing.' Disappearing. For some reason, there is some … force, some … there isn't word for it. All I know is that whatever it is, it can make people vanish, memories vanish. Time vanish."

"Time?"

"In the morning, a house looks like it was built yesterday. In the afternoon, the same house looks like it was built a hundred years ago. All those years in between, the time it would have taken for the decay to have happened, that time ... vanished."

"I think I'm losing my mind."

"Join the club."

Stuart suddenly thought of something. "Wait a minute. I forgot but you didn't. You remembered it all. Why—?"

"The forever and always answer to all *why* questions is going to be 'I don't know' so it's really useless to keep launching them out there into conversations."

"Ok, *what*—?"

"What I have observed is that it's about being *from* Nower County. Being born here. You 'outsiders'—"

"People from Away From Here—"

Cotton smiled a little. "Charlie educated you good. Yes, you flatlanders are subject to a mind sweep."

"And nowhere people are immune?"

He nodded. "I've talked to Shep Clayton about it, though he's not making much sense most of the time. His wife was supposed to show up at the neonatal unit of University Hospital in Lexington to pick him up. He'd stayed the night with their newborn son, who was scheduled to be released. But his wife never showed up. And when Shep went home ... his house, it was one of the old ones. The roof was caved in, old boards holding up a shell of walls. He'd left it the day before — less than twenty-four hours — had sent his wife home to get a good night's sleep, fix up the baby's room — and when he came back all evidence that he or his family had ever been there was gone, blown away and decayed by time."

"Shepherd *Clayton*, you say?" Stuart's mind was spinning.

"He lost it when he saw the house. His family, they're … simple people. They're from waaaay back in the mountains around Poorfolk Hollow near Drayton County. Most of his people lived on the other side of the county line and when they came home, their houses were just like they'd left them. Whatever this is, it's only happening *inside* Nower County. They went to the police, too, tried to report it, didn't get anywhere. And Shep hasn't been right in the head since."

"Shep's wife — her name wouldn't be Abby, would it?"

"Yes, how do you know?"

"Because the name 'Abby *Clayton*' was written on the calendar in Charlie's kitchen, on June fifth or sixth."

Stuart felt himself shiver, but didn't think he actually had, not physically anyway. "It was a reminder … for a *graveside* service. In Charlie's world …" He didn't like saying it like that, but the words fit reality. "Wherever Charlie is, Abby Clayton is *dead*."

Cotton said nothing for a few moments, trying to get his own mind around it. Then he said, "We need to go pay Shep a visit."

"To tell him I believe his wife's dead? How's that going to work?"

"Maybe … we won't have to tell him anything. Maybe he already knows."

Chapter Sixteen

"Hey, it's me," Hayley said when Sugar Bear answered the phone on the third ring.

"Hayley! What are you doing? I told you not to call me. What if Toby'd picked up the phone?"

"I'd have pretended it was a wrong number, or asked to speak to his mother and he'd have told me she—"

"I don't want you talking to Toby about his mother!"

"I wouldn't … why …? What's wrong with you?"

She hadn't meant to make the words an accusation but they'd come out that way and there was some small part of her that was glad she'd stood up to him.

"Wrong with me? Wrong with *me*?" Then he stopped, calmed down. When he spoke again, she could hear the concern in his voice. "We don't need to be talking about what's wrong with me. It's what's wrong with *you* that matters. Did Sam agree to … fix it?"

"Not on the phone."

"Why can't you just tell me—?"

"My mother might come and hear. We have to talk in person. We need to meet."

"I don't have anybody to look after Toby."

"We have to talk." There. She'd done it again, she'd been firm. "Tonight, while my parents are at that county meeting."

"She wouldn't do it, would she?" The question was emotionless, clinical.

"I said I can't talk now."

"That's what I figured." He let out a breath. "Okay, then. Yeah, we need to meet. We absolutely do. I'll pick a place, and let you know."

"What's wrong with behind the Henderson's barn?" The Hendersons were a retired couple who spent almost all their time with their daughter's family in Florida. The barn on the back of their property was secluded, invisible from the road with a spot to park cars where they'd be concealed by large oleander bushes. And inside the barn was a pile of hay where you could spread out a blanket and ...

He paused, seemed to be holding onto his emotions.

"When we meet ... I want it to be somewhere *different*. I'll call, you answer and I'll just say where, and then you can hang up immediately, like it was a wrong number."

Why did he want to pick some new place for them to meet? She wanted to ask, but didn't have the chance.

"I have to go now." And the phone went dead.

Chapter Seventeen

For the first time in his life, E.J. Stephenson had a full appreciation of the suffering of drug addicts. He got it, understood the almost irresistible yearning. Even though he had taken only a few doses of oxycontin — and had been in legitimate need of the drug — that warm, lips tingling, utopian sense of wellbeing it produced was as seductive as a beautiful woman. It was like sex in a lot of ways, in fact. It was as elemental and fundamental as that. The human need, yearning, aching desire was as powerful as the sex drive of an adolescent boy looking at a *Playboy* magazine.

Sam had kept him pretty "doped up," and he was grateful for that, for the relief it provided him from the agony of his leg. But the relief was short-lived. He would usually doze off after Sam gave him one of the little white pills, and when he awoke, the ache had returned to his leg. As the drug wore off, the pain ratcheted up like dialing up the light on a dimmer switch.

He was only able to think clearly in that narrow window of time right after he woke up. The pain was a mere throbbing ache from his knee to his ankle, with spiked throbbing up into his groin. It was bearable and his mind was clear. When the drug made him so dopey, he was unable to find any meaning in his thoughts nor any desire to care. And when the pain was at its zenith, that last few minutes before his next dose of oxi, he was so distracted by the agony that thought was impossible.

He had never known pain like that. Had made it through life mostly uninjured. He had gotten a nasty gash on his arm when he was a senior in high school. It had required thirteen stitches to close and had gotten infected later, which meant he had to go back to the doctor to re-open the wound — hurt like a firebrand — and clean it out. He'd broken a toe slamming it into the leg of the dresser when he was in college. It had turned purple and he had hobbled around for weeks, his friends making fun of the limp and his stubbed toe. And there was the horse bite that had broken a finger.

But there was nothing in E.J.'s life history that would have prepared him for how bad his leg hurt. On a scale of one to ten it was a seventy-five. It was sickening, the agony turned his stomach. Sam had wisely limited his intake to clear liquids because she knew he would not be able to keep much of anything else down.

But during that clear-thinking window — between fuzzy LaLa Land and an agony he did not know could be endured by human beings, in that window of time, he thought about the fact that he was going to die of rabies.

For a while, he had tried unsuccessfully to delude himself into the belief that the lone shot he had taken more than a decade ago would provide him the protection he needed. But he never had been very good at self-deception — not even when he was a kid and had such a crush on Charlie Ryan, *McClintock*, and that he sometimes imagined she had the hots for him, too.

Not.

Unless he could get the anti-rabies shot in … he wasn't sure how much time had passed since he had been mauled, but he didn't think it'd been twenty-four hours yet. Maybe it had, he didn't know. But that deadline would pass soon enough with no first injection, unless the Jabberwock cooperated in a way that right now didn't seem likely, blew back out of here like it had blown in. He didn't believe that would happen. Had reached the same conclusion as Malachi, though they had only discussed it briefly. This wasn't a natural phenomenon or the corruption of a natural phenomenon or the outer extreme of some naturally occurring force on earth. This was other. Outside. It could conceivably back off and leave Nowhere County alone, but E.J. didn't believe that was the game plan. The Jabberwock wasn't going anywhere. And neither was E.J. or anybody else.

No vaccine … rabies.

He had seen a couple of rabid animals during his medical training. A fox and a cat. It was an awful experience. The fox had had dumb rabies. The kind that Buster, unfortunately, did *not* have. Of the two types of rabies, dumb rabies was the most prevalent. An animal with dumb rabies was just disoriented, became unable to walk, to move at all. Eventually, their jaws locked up so they drooled, and then they had a seizure, sometimes more than one, and died.

The cat had had furious rabies, like Buster. It attacked the walls of its cage, trying to chew its way out, broke off its teeth and tore up its mouth but didn't notice or care. Toward the end, it began attacking its own backside, chewed off its own tail and then ran around in circles trying to catch the bleeding stump that was always one step out of its grasp.

It had multiple seizures before it died.

That was coming soon to a theater near E.J.

He thought back on those last moments, with his leg a gushing gory wound he couldn't think beyond, of diving under the power take-off and getting Buster to follow him. Then the world had grayed out. But he had caught sight of Judd's face when Judd found him. The look of horror was imprinted on the back side of E.J.'s brain to reappear there for as long as he lived. Which apparently wouldn't be long. The dog had been mangled by the power take-off so badly it was unrecognizable as a dog, its huge body wrapped around and around the spinning shaft, crushed, stretched out of its skin, all its bones broken. E.J. didn't know if the horror on Judd's face was for the dog or for him.

But the PTO had at least spared Buster the final stages of the disease, the locked jaw and seizures. In humans that stage also featured an unreasoning fear of water, hence the name hydrophobia. Crushed beyond recognition was a horrible way to die, but it had been quick.

And E.J. began to wonder if it would be possible for him to do what Buster had done. Sign out, leave the game before the curtain fell. Was there some way for him to … die without having to suffer through the horror of rabies to do it?

Would one of his friends slip him a lethal dose of oxycontin? So he could plop, plop, fizz, fizz, oh what a relief it is, and then ride off into the sunset on a pink cloud of drug-induced euphoria.

Sounded a lot better than foaming at the mouth and seizures.

Would one of them be willing to do it, to provide him

an escape before the rabies took his mind, will and body and rendered him incapable of escape? If so, which one?

Sam?

Charlie?

Malachi?

Who should he ask?

Chapter Eighteen

The crowd of gawkers was gone. The funeral business that'd failed in Persimmon Ridge years ago was a growing concern now in Nowhere County. Willy Cochran and Abby Clayton on J-Day. Now Martha Whittiker. All in just two weeks.

The old lady had no family here. Somebody would have to take it upon themselves to provide a funeral and burial. Liam didn't know who that would be, given that her only relative in the county was her grandson, who was the prime suspect in her murder.

Except he didn't do it.

Liam certainly was no great detective, but you didn't have to be a rocket scientist to see the scene in Dylan Shaw's apartment had been staged.

Head wounds bled a lot. Liam knew that from his emergency medical technician training. They always looked more serious than they were. Well, unless you could see bone and gray matter, which you couldn't with Martha Whittiker. The wound had bled, though, had to have bled.

And there was almost no blood where the body had been found.

She had been killed somewhere else and her body dumped in Dylan's apartment.

And who would do a thing like that? Liam didn't have any idea but the only safe bet was that it *wasn't* her grandson. Even a wacked-out druggie wouldn't have killed his grandmother and then hauled her body to his own apartment and dumped it on the floor.

So if Martha Whittiker hadn't been killed in her apartment, where had she been killed? All the evidence in the yard and flower beds had been trampled by the gawkers so there was no way to determine if she had been dragged across the yard and gardens. From a car maybe, or from the house.

Liam went to the house and searched it, looking for blood, but found none. What he did find, however, was a kitchen floor so clean you could have performed open-heart surgery on it. And the smell of bleach was almost overwhelming. Unless Martha Whittiker, in her last moments on earth had been cleaning her kitchen floor with bleach, then got up and put the cleaning supplies away—

Put them away. Liam went into the laundry room and quickly found what he was looking for — an empty bottle of bleach stuffed into the trash can. There was a red-brown smudge on the bottle, which he would bet was blood.

It might even be that a fingerprint could be lifted from the smudge. Except Liam didn't have access to finger-printing equipment. A forensics team might have been able to lift prints off the blood on the outside of Dylan Shaw's apartment door, too. But there was no forensics team.

Liam walked slowly from the laundry room back into

the kitchen, the likely scene of a murder, and wondered, as he had wondered countless other times in the past two weeks, what he was supposed to do with this information. Was it his job to try to track down the killer? How on earth would he go about doing that? And if he found the killer …

He shook his head, trying to order his thoughts. His mind seemed to be on a continuous loop going nowhere.

Police training had described that as a phenomenon some law enforcement officers experienced after a trauma on the job. The police officer who keeps his gun trained on the bank robber he just shot, continuing to yell at him to drop his weapon.

Liam's mind wasn't in that kind of loop. It was in a conundrum loop, the one he'd been in since he'd awakened in the bus shelter two weeks ago with a needle inside his skull.

As the lone law enforcement officer in the county, what was he supposed to do … about crime and criminals? He didn't know, hoped tonight's meeting would provide some guidance. But throughout the day, a feeling of dread had been growing in his belly, a sense that something wasn't right, that the meeting was likely to ping off in an entirely unexpected direction that would leave him in worse shape than he had been in before.

One thing he *could* do, though. He could clear Dylan Shaw of suspicion. And he knew where to start looking for the young man. Surely, he had run away from what he'd obviously discovered on his living room floor. If he had, he had become acquainted with the Jabberwock, in which case he had spent time in some state of incapacitation in the Dollar Store parking lot.

Liam would go there and have a talk with Sam or Charlie or Malachi — whoever happened to be at the clinic. Tell them what he'd found in Martha Whittiker's kitchen. Ask them if Dylan had shown up in the Middle of Nowhere and did they know where he went afterward. He'd also ask what they thought Liam should do about the murder. They didn't likely have any more answers than he did, but they'd at least provide moral support. Maybe even help him puzzle it out.

Dylan Shaw hadn't killed his grandmother.

But somebody sure as Jackson had. And who might that be?

Chapter Nineteen

Viola Tackett opened the heavy curtains a crack, just wide enough so she could see out between them. They was so old and dusty she had to hold her breath or she'd have a sneezing fit.

She and the boys had come into West Liberty Middle School through a door on the north side that opened into a space beside the building you couldn't see from the street. The auditorium and the little gymnasium inside the school still remained functional for public use. The school mirrored the architecture of the courthouse and the two buildings sat like bookends in the middle of the block, one on either side of the street, with wide steps and tall white columns and big oversized double doors, inlaid on both sides by leaded glass windows. Parking for the courthouse was out front along both sides of Main Street, each space with its own personal parking meter that hadn't been nothing but lawn art since the Eisenhower Administration. Parking for the school was behind it, where there was a lot, a wide drop-off lane for buses and an overgrown play-ground where the swing set didn't have no swings, the basketball goal didn't have no rim and both seesaws was broke in two. The monkey bars was still there, though. Set in concrete like they was, they'd have survived an atomic bomb blast.

The school building had been spared the vandalism that'd chewed up the other abandoned structures in the county due to its strategic location across the street from the courthouse that housed the sheriff's department. There were plenty of other windows to break out, walls to spray paint, and bridge abutments to deface without risking getting caught by the law. So the building stood mostly untouched, by people, anyway. But time and age and the elements had done plenty of touching, had touched the roof with leaks that'd made huge brown circles on the ceiling high above the auditorium floor where the seats had been removed years ago. The doors were padlocked shut, but anybody'd wanted to get in bad enough coulda done it because the wood in the doors and the jambs was rotting away.

You could hear the crowd out there, but wasn't no gaiety to the sound. Onliest time there was ever that many nowhere people all together in one place was at whoop-ti-doos, and there hadn't been one of them here in twenty years. They'd been a good time, though, them whoop-ti-doos. Mountain folk from all over would gather in some hollow that had a good-sized piece of flat land. Some-body'd dig a big pit, fill it with the right kinda wood — oak and hickory for the heat, cedar for the seasoning — with charcoal on top and there'd be an animal carcass on a spit over the pit, with a crank on the end so's you could turn it slow-like, get it done even on all the sides. There'd also be a bucket with a mop in it so's you could slather what was in the bucket on the meat as it cooked — some special kinda barbecue sauce some granny up in the hills had a recipe for that'd died with her and couldn't nobody ever make it again.

There'd be tables set up somebody'd snatched out of the basement of one of the closed churches, piled high with all kinda food — fried okra, grits, greens, beans cooked with a ham hock, blackberry cobbler — mountain food, and the nature of a "covered-dish" social was such that every cook wanted to out-do every other one, so whatever they brung was the best thing they knew how to make and the whole of it was a feast fit for a king.

Or a queen.

The queen of Nowhere. That's what Viola Tackett was gonna be. Not yet, but soon. Yeah, very soon. Tonight was the beginning of it all.

Tonight's meeting had been called by Sebastian Nower, but the idea'd been Liam Montgomery's and if he hadn't come up with it like he done Viola woulda had to orchestrate that part, too. It was better this way, her not having nothing to do with the meeting, just come here like ever'-body else to try to put they heads together and figure things out. And anything else that happened … well, it was just — what was the word? Spontaneous. Yeah, spontaneous,

She'd come in the door that led to the stage in front of the auditorium so she could make sure all the pieces was in place, all the folks was where they was supposed to be, wanted to check now so's she could fix it if one of the dumb-as-a-brick hillbillies wound up on the wrong side of the room.

Nower was preening like a peacock, so glad to be in charge of something he was like to wet his pants.

Sebastian Nower, who lived in the big three-story house on Hawthorne Lane in the Ridge. One of the last remaining fancy homes that'd once been scattered all over the Ridge and into some of the other communities in the county. Back when things was going well and the Ridge had been a real town and the county wasn't sliding down a greasy slope toward nowhere at all.

She'd set her heart on that house first time she ever seen it more than half a century ago, all decked out like it was for Christmas, with candles in all the windows. And her outside on the street 'cause Mama'd brought the little'uns in so the church could give them Christmas presents their parents couldn't afford. They done that for several poor families ... made them grovel and say thank you and kiss everybody's butt and be properly grateful that them high-and-mighty folks had taken the time out of their busy, important lives to go buy a junk toy from the Five-and-Dime to give to kids who needed a pair of shoes and a warm coat a whole lot worse.

She'd stared up at that house, hadn't never seen nothing in all her six years of drawing breath so grand as it was. And she felt a yearning she didn't even know how to feel because until that time she hadn't never seen nothing in her world worth the wanting of it. But she wanted that, she wanted to be a little girl dressed in a lacy white dress, putting on airs with the kinds of folks who told folks like her what to do.

She'd slipped away then, couldn't help herself, went around the back of the house and peeked in one of the windows where the drapes was open. Just had to get a look, only a peek into such a marvel that she couldn't imagine real people lived there.

Then that fella grabbed her by the ear, worked for the Nower family he did, and yelled at her for trampling the flower bed though it was wintertime and wasn't no flowers growing there. He'd hauled her out to the street and called out,

"This one belong to any of you?"

Her mama had stepped forward to claim her and the man shoved Viola at her, then looked down at his own hand and said, "That child needs a bath!"

He'd glanced around at the handful of people who'd happened to be on the street. "It's no sin to be poor, but soap's cheap."

And they all grinned at each other and at him, signifying that they knew the likes of her could have afforded to be clean if they'd chosen to be, and were dirty because they was just dirty people, that was all. Lowlifes.

The man had informed her mother all haughty-like that she could take her brood and leave, clearly undeserving as they was of the generosity of their betters. They didn't have no Christmas whatsoever 'cause of what she done. It just passed like any other day, and they lived through it like any other one, cold and hungry.

The Nower House was a symbol of all that Viola Tackett shoulda had in her life but didn't, but was gonna finally have now at the end of it, no matter what she had to do or who she had to step on to do it.

Gratified that her peek through the auditorium curtains had revealed that nobody was out of place, she let the curtains fall shut and motioned for the boys to come with her across the stage and out the little door to the auditorium off the side so wouldn't nobody notice. They would make their way to the back of the room so's she would be in place when the show started at 6:30.

Chapter Twenty

Sam kept turning around, craning to see. And her height afforded her some advantage in that endeavor. As the room filled with people, she watched the doorway for Malachi's appearance. Sam had watched out the window of the clinic and saw him and Roscoe Tungate drive away to search for Harry, certain theirs was a hopeless errand. If Harry's house had "aged," it wasn't likely they were going to find Harry out for a stroll or down at the creek fishing.

Harry had vanished.

And what, exactly, did "vanished" mean? If the people were gone, where did they go? And how did they get there? And what did it mean that their houses aged, a process for which Sam had a morbid fascination — a ridiculously creepy desire to watch the transformation, to witness the process. And why those particular people? Abner Riley … okay, he did, after all, live in Fearsome Hollow, and to Sam that one characteristic was enough to explain any out-of-the-ordinary experience. She'd finally gotten to hear the whole story about what had happened when Charlie,

Malachi and the Tungates went there looking for Abner. The mist. The sparkling black forms. Whispers. Wails. The car *picked up and moved!*

But Harry Tungate didn't live in Fearsome Hollow. Neither did Reece Tibbits. Liam had gotten sidetracked *by a murder,* and hadn't yet had time to tell Grace that her son, daughter-in-law and two granddaughters were … gone.

Rodney Sentry, the pig farmer who'd stayed at the Middle of Nowhere to help out on J-Day, was missing, too. He lived with his elderly mother on a farm on Oldham Pike in Sawmill Hollow. Liam said the house now looked a hundred years old. And the Crumps. Willard and Ethel lived on Wiley Road on the other side of the covered bridge. Ethel'd stayed hidden in their basement the first week after J-Day, but had promised her sister Margaret she'd help her finish up a quilt two days ago. When Ethel didn't show up, Margaret sent her husband, Willie, to check and he'd said the Crump house had become a dilap-idated shack. Or so said Margaret, who'd told her neighbor Agnes Wheatley, who'd told her cousin, Gladys Copley, who had told her best friend, Effie Bennett, who had told her niece Raylynn, who had told Sam this morning at the clinic.

It was possible Abby Clayton's had been the first house to undergo the transformation. After she … died, a couple of her sisters and a brother — her mother was dead and her wack-job father was blessedly out of the county — had gone to her house. Certainly not to find something to dress her in for the funeral, which was *not* an open casket affair. And they'd reported — hysterically, as Sam heard it from Liam — that Abby and Shep's little house in Poorfolk Hollow was not the house Abby had left the morning of J-Day to buy onesies at the Dollar General Store.

Charlie and Merrie appeared at Sam's side. Rusty had

not come with Sam to the meeting, begged off with some excuse that was clearly an excuse and they both knew it. He didn't want to go and she wouldn't force him, but she would do her best to force out of him later why he hadn't wanted to attend. The boy was withdrawn, seemed to have been pulling away from her ever since ... No, that wasn't fair. His response to the craziness was certainly a normal one and she needed to give him space and "permission" to feel whatever he was feeling. And she needed to spend more time with him, be available for when he opened up. More time than what she'd squeezed into this afternoon. She was neglecting her son — she *was!* And whenever the realization struck her she was remorseful and ashamed. And vowed to do better. But then another emergency ...

"You're easy to pick out in a crowd," Charlie told her, gesturing at her red hair. "You'd make a lousy 'Where's Waldo?'"

"Have you seen Malachi, heard anything about Harry Tungate?"

"No and no."

"Why couldn't I stay at the click-click?" Merrie asked Charlie. Click-click was her word for the animal clinic. "I wanted to play wiff the puppies!" Then she stuck out her lip in a pout. When that little girl turned on the charm she was absolutely irresistible, but she was clearly a "strong-willed child," a handful, and Sam suspected Charlie had once been better at reining her in. Sam knew the experience of believing the child was dead still haunted Charlie, though, and she gave the child more rope than she should have.

"I told you, honey. Miss Raylynn is busy looking after E.J. She doesn't have time to babysit you, too."

"I need to go potty."

Charlie rolled her eyes at Sam and led the child off into the crowd.

The room was filling up fast. Everyone was standing, of course, because the auditorium seats had been removed after someone tried to set them on fire years ago and they'd never been replaced. Why bother?

Why bother? The words hung on a nail in Sam's head. That seemed to be the knee-jerk response to just about everything that was broken in the whole county. Why bother? Nobody cared.

Somehow that set off a soft, clanging alarm in Sam's head. Maybe she'd missed her calling as an advertising copywriter.

The slogan for the Jabberwock: When you dial 911, nobody comes.

The slogan for Nowhere County: Why bother?

She had never before given consideration to how folks felt about Nowhere County. It was the canvas on which all their lives were painted: why bother? In some convoluted way she couldn't explain, she had a niggling suspicion that the sentiment expressed by the slogan had come back to bite all of them in the butt.

There'd been seating for 600 in the auditorium, so without seats the same space could easily accommodate twice that many. And if folks jammed in around where the seats had been, in the aisles and the back of the room … there was definitely enough space for any county residents who wanted to attend.

Viola Tackett and three of her boys appeared out the door from backstage. She wondered how much Malachi was involved in his mother's businesses. He had come home so "disabled" from Rwanda, she got the sense that he didn't do much of anything. Which begged the question: Did Viola know Malachi was going to speak tonight?

If so, did she know what he was going to say? Had they talked about it? She suspected not.

Turning around, she scanned the people coming through the two big doors in the back of the room. She spotted Rev. Norman and his wife Sophie and wondered if Hayley'd yet told them she was pregnant. Not likely. The couple was as somber as everybody else, far too composed for parents who'd just found out their sixteen-year-old daughter was going to have a baby.

The crowd had been "summoned" the same way they'd been warned about the Jabberwock. Phone trees almost explained it, but not quite. Sometimes Sam believed in the hundredth monkey … the philosophy that if ninety-nine monkeys know a thing the other one will know it too, just because the rest do. Mountain folk were intensely clannish, stuck to their own, *their* hollow, *their* mountain, *their* families. But if the lines were drawn between mountain folk and the rest of the world, they'd all line up together on the same side. The Jabberwock had done that to them.

The old voice of the public address system, that, in Sam's memory, had never turned on without the awful feedback squawk, focused everyone's eyes on the front of the room. Liam Montgomery was there standing beside Sebastian Nower, who had chosen his attire for the occasion as if he had come to be presented an Oscar. She knew Liam planned to rein in the old man before he could get on a roll, had seemed confident that he could manage it when he'd stopped by the clinic earlier with the bad news about Martha Whittiker. The old woman's murder — *murder!* — had galvanized his determination to assert his legal authority. And his moral authority. He was "the law" and Sam knew he intended to man up to that responsibility.

The only question was: could he pull it off?

"Good evening, folks, thanks for coming," Liam said into the squawky microphone.

Charlie and Merrie rejoined Sam, who craned her neck at the doors.

Where was Malachi?

Chapter Twenty-One

Sugar Bear was *so sweet!*

Hayley'd gotten a lump in her throat as soon as he told her where he wanted her to meet him. The overlook, where they had first made love.

She sucked in a strangled sob. She had never loved anyone in her life as much as she loved Sugar Bear. And he loved her, too. If not for the Jabberwock, they could have continued to see each other. She had fantasies she didn't tell him about. In her best true heart, she believed that they were soul mates, destined to be together, and the universe would not allow them to remain apart. She would turn eighteen in just twenty-one months. And once she was of age, she could make her own decisions. They could be together then.

But all that had been before the pregnancy test.

Things were different now.

She passed the sign for the Scott's Ridge Overlook and looked at her watch. He'd told her to meet him here at 6:30 and she was right on time. Taking a trembling breath, she let it out slowly. She had to be strong. He would want her to be strong and she would do that. It would be her gift to him, her strength as she raised their child alone. Just like in the movies.

She was grateful to the Jabberwock that it kept his wife away. Edna had been out of town on J-Day, which left Sugar Bear alone. Well, except for his little boy. If she could have gotten the procedure done, everything would have worked out. With his wife gone, they could meet whenever they wanted, be together as much as they wanted. But now … when her father found out she was pregnant, she would never be with Sugar Bear again. Well, not never, but not for years.

Maybe that's what they would talk about today.

A little bloom of hope grew in her chest.

That's why he'd picked here, why he'd wanted to see her here, in their special place! He was going to pledge his love for her, tell her he would wait for her. That it was only twenty-one months, and he'd be there on the other side — oh, that really was like a movie! No one would know of their love but the two of them, their passionate secret, and when she turned eighteen, she would announce to her family that she was leaving and she and Sugar Bear and their precious love child would be together forever. And his little boy, too, of course. Toby.

Sugar Bear might not remember it, but the first time they'd met, it had been because of Toby. She had been teaching one of the classes in the church's Vacation Bible School. She'd been a child herself then, only thirteen, and it was before she had started putting on all the weight. Sugar Bear had come to pick up Toby, who was a strange little boy, frightened of his own shadow.

A niggling little memory surfaced before she could bat it back down. She'd been teaching a lesson on prayer and asked the children to describe what they prayed about.

Toby hadn't wanted to join in, but she had prodded him until he blurted out, "God doesn't answer prayers. I begged him to make Daddy stop hurting Mommy but he didn't help."

Of course, that was before she knew Sugar Bear. You only had to look into his eyes to know he would never harm anybody.

She saw the overlook sign up ahead and she felt a little shiver down her spine. She would never have dreamed when she came here just a few months ago, how a chance encounter here would change her life forever.

SHE CAN'T CRY YET, *not now. If she cries now it will wash out her contact lenses so she can't see and she has to be able to drive. She will hold it in until she gets there, where she can let go of all the pain and hurt, make as much noise as she wants and nobody will hear.*

Just a few chance words. "Aw, come on. The party will suck and you know it."

"Seriously. Who wants to watch Hayley-Whaley blow out sixteen candles? The thought turns my stomach."

Ginger, Whitney and Sophia were washing their hands and didn't know Hayley was in the last bathroom stall. She'd pulled her feet up when they came in, didn't want them to know she was there because she knows she's going to make a really bad stink. She'll hold it until they leave. She has always suffered from terrible gas; the doctor says that's part of her overall "metabolic" problem, why she puts on weight, why she can't lose, something about the way her body processes food. And when she has a bowel movement — the reek is staggering.

"She's gross," Whitney says. "All those rolls of fat. And when she eats—"

Ginger giggles. "Yeah, the pig noises — snort, snort. She'll probably shove the whole birthday cake in her mouth in one bite."

"If she weren't Pastor Norman's daughter—" Sophia puts in.

"But she is."

"She makes me nauseous."

"Don't eat any solid food before the party." Ginger giggles again. "Just 'clear liquids' — in case you throw up."

Hayley had held it until they left, then let fly with the most awful stinky, noxious fumes that gagged her ... while she sat there trying not to burst into tears. Then she'd gotten in Daddy's car, didn't even ask if she could use it, and came roaring out to The Top of the World. That's what Hayley calls Scott's Ridge Overlook. It is a spot high on the side of Ironwood Mountain in Dragon Root Hollow. A cliff face that provides a breathtaking view of the hollow and the Rolling Fork River two hundred feet below. Sometimes teenagers parked down the little piece of road where you could park in the trees and nobody could see you, a good place to screw in the car. But it was the middle of the day and there wouldn't be anybody there.

There is a winding path that leads to the spot where somebody — maybe the state road department years ago — had built a security fence that now dangles down off the cliff, like a raveled string on a sweater. The last post had been sunk in concrete too deep for vandals to destroy it and the rest of the fence hangs down from it. There's an old concrete picnic table that's too heavy to move or somebody would have thrown it off the bluff, too.

She comes here often because it is remote, the forest growing out to the edge of the cliff muffles sound so it's her favorite place to let go, sob loud — like she can't do at home or Daddy will tell her to pray about it and everything will be fine.

She parks in the pull-off on the shoulder of the nameless gravel road that leads to the overlook from Crocket Pike and walks down the path to the overlook. That's why she's so surprised when she sees someone sitting on the picnic table, on the table, feet on the stone seat. He must have parked in the lot ... she turns to hurry back to her car but he has seen her.

It's Mr. Witherspoon, the man who owns the Dollar General Store in the Middle of Nowhere.

"If you came to be by yourself," he says as he gets down off the table, "I was just leaving." Then he recognizes her.

"Oh, hello, Hayley."

"Hi Mr. Witherspoon, and you don't have to leave because of me, I'll just—"

"You came here to be by yourself, didn't you?" He hangs his head. "I get it. That's why I came here, too."

The kindness and understanding in his voice are more than she can stand. She bursts into tears, doesn't mean to but she has been holding onto the emotional outburst for so long she can no longer control it. He rushes to her side and puts his arm around her shoulder and the next thing she knows she's clinging to him sobbing … and then …

The rest just … happens. Neither of them planned it. He takes her virginity while she lies naked before him on the cold concrete of the picnic table, right out in the open where anybody who comes along can see, but theirs is such passionate, wild abandon they don't even care.

Afterwards, he's not awkward with her. Helps her get dressed, touches her tenderly in places no one has ever touched her as he does. She had never known she possessed such passion.

He only becomes awkward when he asks if he can see her again. And she begs, breathlessly, "Yes, please. Again and again and again."

He laughs, that wonderful, gentle laugh.

THAT NIGHT when she got home, she was so consumed with emotion she had to pour out her feelings in her journal, writing so fast the ink smeared in places, described the whole thing. Well, not the *real* thing. Just what she *wished* had happened, what she fantasized. The tall dark stranger who found her there alone and ravished her, ripped her clothes away in a frenzy of uncontrolled desire, took her virginity as she looked up at him through her tears. She described his rugged face, his shock of unruly black hair and piercing blue eyes. She could see him as clearly as she had seen Mr. Witherspoon because she had been dreaming of him her whole life. Well, versions of him. For a while he looked like Brad Pitt, the way he looked as that hitchhiker in *Thelma & Louise*. Then he became Pierce Brosnan as James Bond. In fact, as Mr. Witherspoon was … doing it … she closed her eyes and pictured him, her dark stranger, the mat of black hair on his chest glistening with sweat as he took her. She always pictured him, every time. Of course, she never told Sugar Bear that.

And she never again journaled about their meetings. In truth, she had never felt the need to journal about anything after Sugar Bear came into her life and shined light into all the dark places. She would journal about today, though, their last time together, because she was sure it would be heartbreaking, lovers torn out of each other's arms. It would be just like that final scene in *Casablanca*. Rick made Ilsa leave him, sacrificed his own happiness, denied himself his only chance at true love. Maybe Sugar Bear would do that — send her away, deny himself. Or maybe she should.

This time, Hayley parked in the secluded lot. Sugar Bear's car was already there. He had come early because he was so anxious to see her! That butterfly feeling fluttered in her belly just like it always did before she saw him. They would make love today. She'd come prepared, had taken a shower and put on her best perfume, dabbed it between her breasts where he liked to snuggle his nose. They would make love and talk about what the future might bring for both of them. And maybe it wasn't all bad. Maybe Sugar Bear had their future all planned out.

Chapter Twenty-Two

Sam was proud of Liam Montgomery. He had manned up since the day he sat in the bus shelter, moaning softly about the "needle" in his head. Even though he'd been low man on the totem pole in the sheriff's department before J-Day, he had accepted law enforcement responsibility for the county, and his uniform alone stood for something, gave a sense of assurance that there was somebody here who was in charge and knew what they were doing.

That sense had been waning as the days stacked up one on top of the other, though. It had taken flight alongside the belief that whatever the Jabberwock was, they'd wake up in the morning and it'd be gone just like they'd awakened to find its shimmering presence surrounding the county two weeks ago.

After all, it was only temporary, right? And if you didn't cross it — literally — it only mattered when it was important to get out of the county or to get something in. Most people believed that the Jabberwock itself was harmless — after all, it was just some bizarre meteorological anomaly that'd blown in and would soon blow back out and they could go on with their lives.

It was, wasn't it?

"I don't have to tell anybody in this room that something is happening here to all of us that has changed everything in our lives. We've all been dealing with it individually, in our own ways, but I believe it's time for us to figure out how we, all of us, as nowhere people need to respond as a group, doing together what none of us can do individually."

Sebastian Nower stepped up beside Liam then and literally pushed him away from the microphone. Liam probably wasn't expecting such rudeness from the old man, and was too polite to confront it; after all, the old man was near eighty and maybe some key synapses weren't firing anymore.

"Thank you, son," he said dismissively, and turned back to the crowd. "I know you people are looking for guidance and assistance in this time of our mutual need and the Nower family has for generations taken seriously its responsibility to the people in the county we founded when a contingent of settlers came through the Cumberland Gap to stake their claim in the settlement called Nower's Trace more than two hundred years ago."

And he was off to the races.

He was an imposing figure, she'd give him that. He'd been tall and broad-shouldered in his youth — all of which he spent in schools or elsewhere outside the county that was his family's namesake. But the years had shrunken him, bent his back and taken the meat and muscle off his bones. Standing at the microphone in a business suit so he looked like he had just ducked out of some *important* board meeting during which *important* people would discuss *important* things, but he had deigned to surrender a little of this *important* time to lead the Great Unwashed out of the desert and into the Promised Land.

The suit hid his slat-thin frame, sharp elbows and shoulders, set below a face with gaunt cheeks and a flesh-less chin that resembled the knob of a femur. His was the wind-scoured, sun-weathered skin of a cowboy or a sea captain. He was neither, of course, had merely spent a life-time ignoring his dermatologist's warning not to lay out on the beach too long.

But he could not hide the signature attribute of the Nower family, clearly passed on to him by a recessive gene — an Adam's apple more prominent than his nose. You could amuse yourself while he droned on by watching it bob up and down in his skinny neck like the cork on a fishing line.

Sebastian McFarland Nower III was an eccentric whose every statement was taken with enough salt to crust the rims of a million margarita glasses. To his credit, Liam was in the process of taking back the meeting Nower had hijacked when the chaos broke out — from different parts of the room at the same time, like a spark had lit fuses in several places at once.

"There's a murderer loose out there roaming around free as the breeze," called out a woman from the far side of the room whose voice had the distinctive caw of a crow. No, a rooster — Wilma Thacker. "He's preying on older women all alone in the world 'thout no man to protect and defend them. I want to know what the *deputy sheriff's* doing to catch him."

Liam tried to respond but he was shouted down by another voice from the other side of the room.

"A man who'd kill his own kin like that, smash her head in so's you couldn't even recognize—"

"Martha Whittiker's head was not—"

"Martha Whittiker! Somebody killed Martha Whittiker?"

"You saying she's *dead*?"

"Who'd a'done a thing like that to the poor little—?"

"That worthless grandson of hers, that's who," said Ethel Porter, another of Martha's neighbors. "I keep this here loaded gun right by my bed." She waved the pistol in the air as casually as a pompom at a football game. It occurred to Sam then that Ethel wasn't the only person in the crowd with a weapon. Probably half the people in the room were packing. Guns and this kind of tension — a dangerous combination. "I gonna lock my doors, too, ever night now and I ain't never done that before."

Voices began to pop off like popcorn heated up in a skillet.

"Need to string him up."

"Hanging's too good for him."

"Beat your own grandma to death with a claw hammer, he'd ought to—"

"It ain't like he's got anywhere to run to. Oughta be easy for Liam to find—"

"I'm not looking for Dylan Shaw. I don't believe he—"

"You ain't even *lookin'* for him?"

"A man who'd club his little old grandmother to death and you ain't gonna protect us from him?"

"He ain't the only one's gonna do murder," called a male voice from the back and the crowd turned to look. It was George Gribbins. Sam'd heard he'd tried to stand up to Viola the day she took over Foodtown and she'd put him in his place. "Bobby Joe don't give me back my hay rake, I'm gonna—"

"*Yore* hay rake?" Bobby Joe Mattingly responded. "A fella don't get to keep a thing after he done *sold* it to somebody else."

"I never sold you a dang thing!"

"You think them chickens I traded was early Christmas presents?"

"You didn't *trade* me no chickens! Betty Ann paid you for them chickens."

"Chickens ain't the onliest thing George Gribbins and his kin's took." That was Buford Haywood, who'd lost an eye and part of his nose in a mining accident and wore a black eyepatch like a pirate. "If another one of my sheep goes missing—"

"You accusing me of stealing a sheep? What would I want—?

"Well, *somebody* took it. And you's the last one—"

"Musta been Bobby Joe 'cause a man who'd steal a hay rake would steal—"

The sound had ratcheted up in no time into a full-bore shouting match. The Gribbins family — maybe a dozen of them had shown up at the meeting — were yelling at the Mattinglys and the Haywoods. And in less time than it took to tell about it, others were choosing sides in the dispute, threatening all manner of violence.

Charlie shot Sam a frightened look, reached down and puled Merrie up into her arms, turned and headed for the door. Sam looked longingly past her to the empty doorway. Where was Malachi? He could get control of this—

Then George lunged at Bobby Joe, throwing a round-house punch that if it had connected might have severed B.J.'s head from his shoulder blades. But for all his strength, George was slow, and Bobby Joe dodged the blow and threw himself at George.

"You keep your hands off my brother," cried Carl Gribbins. "I'm a'snatch the lot of you baldheaded—"

"—come get my hay rake—"

"Musta been who busted that fence line. I knowed it was a Haywood done it."

The jostling crowd had become a mob in seconds, an angry mob. Maybe it was just-below-the-surface fear of what was happening to them, the pent-up frustration of being locked in.

The bomb had gone off so suddenly, men were fighting everywhere, throwing punches, wrestling on the floor, yelling and cursing and kicking. It was impossible to tell who was on whose side. Those who'd chosen not to take anybody's side in the brawl had been pushed to the sides and back of the room. From a vantage point against the back wall, Sam saw Liam leap off the stage, and begin shoving his way through the crowd to get to the tangle of men throwing punches.

"... put that gun down!" Liam's voice rang out above the cacophony of voices. "All of you, put your guns away—"

Bam!

The gunshot was like a howitzer going off in the confined space of the auditorium. The crowd gasped as one, shocked into silence by the sound.

Suddenly, Sam was afraid. The people were backing up away from something. She was tall and strong and she shoved smaller people out of the way, until she came to the spot where the crowd had parted, away from the body of a man lying face-down on the floor. It was Liam Montgomery, his own pistol beside his limp hand, blood spreading out in a puddle around him.

Sam knelt beside him and he looked up at her with wide, beseeching eyes. Blood formed in the bubbles on his lips when he tried to speak and ran in a trickle out the side of his mouth and down his cheek.

Before Sam even had a chance to find where he'd been

shot, somebody stumbled into her, knocking her over on top of Liam's body.

"Who shot Liam?"

"Wasn't me!"

"Me neither."

"*You* was the one. You and your worthless brothers, a bunch of bottom-feeding—"

The yelling became a single big roar of sound that Sam ignored while she tried to get back onto her hands and knees. But the crowd had closed in around them. She saw someone step on Liam's hand, someone kicked her in the thigh and—

Bam!

Another shot rang out, followed by two more.

The crowd was shocked into silence.

"Next person touches a weapon, I will put you down soon's I would a lame horse."

The voice was stern and vicious. Viola Tackett.

At some point in the riot, and that's what it had degenerated into, Viola had moved to the front of the room and up onto the stage. She stood there now with a rifle in her hands. A rifle! Where did she get a *rifle?* She hadn't been armed with it when Sam saw her and the boys enter the room.

With her cheek on the stock, Viola swept the barrel back and forth over the crowd, ready to pull the trigger.

Every person in the room knew that Viola Tackett would drop them in their tracks with no more concern than swatting a fly. Her oldest son, Neb, was beside her, holding a pistol in a two-hand grip like the cops on television. Obie stood at one corner of the stage, Zach stood at the other — all pointing weapons out into the crowd. They were arranged so perfectly, it looked like they'd rehearsed the drill.

The crowd was totally outgunned and knew it. Nobody would go up against the whole Tackett clan, every one of them as likely to put a hole in you as the next. From their position on the stage, they could have taken out a SWAT team or a squad of Navy SEALs.

"All them weapons, on the floor, *now,*" Viola demanded, and maybe a dozen people leaned over and placed all manner of firepower on the floor in front of them. "Now get back away so Miss Sheridan can see to Liam."

Sam felt the crush of the crowd around her pull away as everyone hurried to do exactly what Viola Tackett had directed. Sam sat back up onto her knees, trying to get a look at Liam in the sudden light that now replaced the forest of legs around her.

Liam's eyes were no longer pleading, beseeching. They stared out sightlessly, the pupils fixed.

Sam let out a little cry, couldn't help it, and the scream was echoed all around the room, handed from one woman to the next, though most didn't know what it was they were screaming at.

"Liam!" she cried, her husky voice suddenly tear-clotted. But there was no response. She put her fingers to his neck, feeling for the pulse, the rhythmic thumping of the carotid artery, echoing the rhythm of his beating heart. But Liam Montgomery gave off no pulse to echo. It was still.

Sam looked up at Viola, who stood with her cheek to the stock of her rifle, ready to fire, and spoke into the startled silence.

"He's dead," Sam said, then sloughed off her professional detachment like dropping a shawl off her shoulders. She leaned over his body, put her arms around him and began to cry.

Chapter Twenty-Three

Sugar Bear was seated on the picnic table, with his feet on the concrete bench beside it, looking just like he did the first time she saw him here. The image took her breath way and she couldn't stifle a sob. He turned and looked at her then, didn't say anything, just got to his feet and held out his arms and she rushed into them.

She cried there for a long time, just as she had done the first time she met him here. But he didn't touch her, slide his hand tantalizingly up her back to unhook her bra strap. Her breasts were large, D cups, heavy and pendulous, and when he had fondled them, she understood for the first time what it meant to be aroused. She'd been panting then, gasping for air, and when he'd leaned over and kissed her there, each one, she would have collapsed from desire if she hadn't been leaning against the table.

Now, he only held her while she cried, patting her back tenderly. She wanted his tenderness, of course, but she needed his passion. She needed to know he still wanted her, still loved her. She needed to feel his presence inside her.

But she *did have* his presence inside her. Carried his baby under her heart. And that's what they had met to talk about. What that meant for both their futures.

She struggled to control her sobbing, knew that her tears had totally destroyed her makeup, that her mascara was running in twin black lines down her cheeks and if she wiped it, it would smear and she'd look like a Halloween mask. she shouldn't have cried, didn't want him to see her like this, their last time.

Last time.

The words threatened to send her into another round of near-hysterical bawling, but she grabbed hold of her emotions. She needed to be strong now. He would want her to be strong. And she had to show him, demonstrate to him that she could be strong … could remain silent and stoic while he waited for her.

Somehow he had guided her to one of the benches attached to the table, facing out, looking out at the view from the Top of the World, only a few feet from the post that held the dangling remains of the restraining fence.

He sat beside her and she pulled out of his arms, wishing for all the world that she'd thought to bring tissues. Why hadn't she thought about that; she had known she was going to cry. But she hadn't and could do nothing better than to lift the hem of her Eastern Kentucky University tee-shirt and use it to wipe the black off her face.

She was surprised that he didn't reach out and touch her as she wiped her face, raising the shirt up over her breasts in a tantalizing display.

Then she took a shaky breath and just looked at him, looked into his face, looking for the love that softened his features when he looked at her. He was not a physically attractive man at all. Narrow shoulders, a sunken white chest and a paunch that sometimes got in the way of their lovemaking — his belly and her belly together. Unless she just lay on her back with her knees drawn up ... the fit was not ideal.

He walked funny. Actually, she had noticed that the first time she met him, the day he came to pick up Toby from Vacation Bible School. He had a bad knee that sometimes just folded up under him and he had developed a hitching sort of gait to compensate, not a limp exactly. A limp would not have looked odd and his — *lurching* — did.

His forehead was too high, and now that his hairline had receded off it, it seemed to loom over the top of his face like a cliff. His black eyebrows grew in a single bristly line across the bridge of his nose and he never trimmed them, so they always looked unruly and unkempt. His nose was too big for his face by half, the most dominant feature above his thin lips and small chin, and the nostrils flared out when he breathed, making it look even bigger. It was also so covered with blackheads, some of them huge, that it looked like he'd spilled pepper on it.

Why was she just noticing that now? Surely she had seen them before. Several of them actually had little black stickery things poking out. If you rubbed your hand across the skin you could have *felt* them. The urge to reach out and squeeze them was almost overpowering. His eyes were small and dark, like little marbles with no discernible color — just dark brown that blended in with the iris so you couldn't even see the black spot in the center.

There was an unreadable look in those eyes right now that was — not alarming, but ... it was just not what she expected to see there.

"Sam said no, didn't she?" he asked, his voice oddly devoid of any emotion.

"She said she wasn't trained to do a ... procedure like

that. But she said that even if she had been, she'd have refused." She drew in a shaky breath. "She said ... it wasn't just, you know, a clump of cells. That it was a baby, and she wouldn't kill it."

He had visibly winced when she said the word 'baby." But maybe he just hadn't realized that she was far enough along — that it really was a baby now.

"She was right. It is ..." She hadn't admitted this even to herself, heard the truth of it in her voice as she said the word. "I've felt it move." She had resolutely ignored the little fluttery feelings, told herself it was just her gurgling gut, her faulty digestive organs that had doomed her to life in a body encased in rolls of fat. Now, she placed her hand almost protectively over her belly.

"Did you tell Sam about me?"

"Sure, I told—"

"Did you tell her *my name*?"

He barked the words and she flinched at his brusqueness.

"No, I called you 'Sugar Bear,' like we agreed."

"Who else knows?"

"Nobody."

"You didn't tell a girlfriend, confide in one of the people in your church?"

"Of course not. You know I don't have any real friends. I don't have anybody ... only you."

She hadn't meant for that last part to sound so plaintive, so pleading. And when he didn't respond with reassurance — that she *did* have him, that he would love her and — she suddenly felt the bottom drop out of her belly.

Could it be ... could it possibly be that he was ... going to leave her? The very thought of it made her so nauseous bile rose up in the back of her throat. It was one thing for their love to be ripped apart by circumstances, two lovers who couldn't be together. That happened in the movies and in stories all the time. It was a horrible thought — not to see him or touch him. But it didn't feel alone. Abandoned. That was the most awful feeling in the world.

"Howie ..."

"I told you not to call me that. Not to ever call me that. You might slip and—"

He must have seen how devastated she felt, read it on her face, because he softened.

"But it's alright. It doesn't matter now. Everything's going to be fine."

She should have felt encouraged by those words. But she didn't. She felt ... frightened.

Chapter Twenty-Four

As soon as the mood of the crowd turned ugly, Charlie carried Merrie out of the room in her arms. She stopped just outside the center set of doors, ready to rush the child to safety outside at the first hint that the chaos in the room was about to spill out of it into the hallway.

She had seen it all, watched in fascinated horror as the docile crowd had been whipped into a frenzy and then goaded into violence. That's what it had looked like to her. The whole encounter hadn't taken five minutes, and the level of hostility had increased in that time from zero to sixty. It had turned mean and ugly almost between one heartbeat and another, and the hostility was not confined to one place in the crowd with a couple of antagonists squaring off at each other. It was everywhere, like a grass-fire that'd been lit in several places at the same time.

The tension in the room now felt like a thunderstorm building up to that first blinding flash of lightening.

Liam jumped off the stage and waded into the crowd, shouting, but his voice was drowned out by—

A gunshot! Abrupt silence.

From where she stood, Charlie couldn't tell if anybody had been shot or if somebody had just fired a shot into the ceiling. But the crowd pulled back from a space in the front left of the crowd like a wave receding off the beach and she saw Sam, the top of her head and her red hair, shove her way through the crowd to that spot and then drop out of sight.

Somebody *had* been shot.

"Who shot Liam?" somebody cried.

Liam? No!

An instantaneous argument broke out, accusations, shouting; the wave that had receded away from the body on the floor instantly flowed back into the space and the opening vanished.

"It was *them!* The good-for-nothing Haywoods."

"Don't you dare accuse—"

Charlie was frozen in shock and horror when another shot rang out, then two more in rapid succession. She turned in the direction of the sounds and saw Viola Tackett and three men — her boys — standing on the stage with weapons trained on the crowd.

Viola had been at the back of the room. Charlie had seen her come out of the little door beside the stage and make her way to the back wall. She hadn't been carrying a rifle then, Charlie was sure of it. But she had one now, trained on the crowd.

In the stunned silence that followed the gunshots, Viola ordered the crowd to put their weapons on the floor, and Sam saw men and women lean over to obey the command. Then she told the crowd to get back so Sam could tend to Liam and directed her boys to collect the firearms. Obie and Zach leapt off the stage to comply. Neb stood stalwartly beside his mother.

Liam!

Seconds ticked by. Only a handful of seconds. Charlie recognized the voice that squeaked out a small scream. It was Sam. Charlie's voice joined the voices of other women in the crowd. Charlie took a couple of steps to go to Sam and Liam before it registered with her that she had Merrie in her arms, whose eyes where huge and frightened.

"Gimme the little 'un," said a voice beside her and she turned to see Mrs. Throckmorton, the woman whose cat had been a patient of E.J.'s on Jabberwock Day. The woman had hovered over her cat and had made friends with Merrie when the child took over the veterinary hospital and turned it into her own personal petting zoo.

"You 'member me, doncha, sweetheart?"

"Mittens!" Merrie said.

Mrs. Throckmorton held out her arms to the child.

"Whadda ya say you and me go outside and I'll show you how to put a June bug on a piece of string and fly it around your head like a model airplane."

Merrie leaned toward the dumpy little woman, her arms extended.

"June bugs go bzzzzz." Merrie made a reasonable facsimile of the cry of a June bug.

"You sound just like one!" She took Merrie out of Charlie's arms and nodded with her chin toward the space on the floor where Liam Montgomery's body lay. "You come get her outside when your … bidness here is done."

Charlie tried to say thank you, but discovered her throat was too clogged to speak. The woman nodded and waddled toward the outside door with Merry babbling cheerfully in her arms.

She didn't remember crossing the room to Liam and Sam, shoving her way through the crowd, mercilessly elbowing anybody who denied her passage.

Bursting out of the crowd, she found Sam on her knees beside Liam, bent over him, holding him. Crying.

She knelt beside Sam, reached out and took Liam's lifeless hand and put her arm around Sam's shoulders.

Viola Tackett was talking now, but Charlie didn't pay any attention to her, shocked, staggered by the sudden violent death of her friend. Later she would remember how Viola had said she would find out who it was that'd shot Liam Montgomery and "see they got theirs," whatever that meant. Then she said she and her boys were going to stand in the gap for the fallen officer, would keep the peace, "land with both feet" on anybody who done something against their neighbors.

"You got a dispute with your neighbor, you come see me," she said. "I'll judge fair, settle things without nobody getting up in somebody else's face. But if'n you decide to settle your own arguments, you're gonna get a little visit from one of my boys."

Her boys. Malachi. Charlie looked around stupidly into the crowd, like he would miraculously appear there. He had agreed to meet her and Sam here at the meeting. The three of them had mapped out what Malachi was going to say, knew people would listen to him even if they didn't like what he was saying. He was, after all, one of Viola Tackett's boys.

But Malachi hadn't shown up. She couldn't imagine what could be important enough to keep him away, because *somebody* had to tell the crowd the information he'd intended to impart.

Somebody.

Charlie got to her feet and called out, "I have something to say." She interrupted Viola right in the middle of her little speech. That did not sit well with Viola, who turned to look at her like she was a little kid who had just wet her pants in church.

"And what might that be, missy …?"

Charlie turned her back on Viola Tackett to address the rest of the crowd.

"I'm Charlie McClintock. Charlene *Ryan* McClintock."

And after those two words of wisdom, Charlie couldn't think of any way in the world to say the rest of what needed to be said.

Chapter Twenty-Five

Hayley would have reached out her hand and touched Sugar Bear's face — she'd done it often, a tender touch that spoke a love she couldn't put into words. But she wasn't certain anymore that he would welcome the touch. And besides, she didn't *want* to touch his face. His nose. How could she possibly have looked at him for months and never noticed, oh by the way, that you could scrape blackheads off his nose with your fingernail. Yuk! She only barely kept herself from shuddering.

She leaned back away from him, aware that her body language was not open and engaging but she couldn't help it.

"What are we going to do?" She kept almost all the emotion out of the question.

"Do?"

"About the baby?"

"Apparently there isn't anything we can do now — about the baby, anyway."

That was an odd thing to say.

Hayley's emotions were suddenly so tangled up, she

had no idea what she felt anymore. She had come here hoping/believing he was going to pledge to her his undying love, tell her he would wait for her, no matter how long it took.

It seemed clear now, he wasn't going to say that.

And she felt … what?

Right now she was … *glad.*

How could she be glad? She couldn't explain it, but something profound had shifted, and she didn't really want him to say he'd wait for her, that they'd be together forever. She didn't want to be with him forever.

It was a thought she had not entertained even momentarily since the day she'd felt the cold concrete on her back on this picnic table, caught up in the heat of passion.

The thought of a future with Howard Witherspoon suddenly didn't sound appealing at all. And there was a certain relief in the realization that there wasn't likely to be one.

But she was going to have his baby.

"I'm keeping it, the baby." She tried to read his expression, but there was a wall up and his face was no longer "the mirror of his soul." It had become the bank vault door that kept everybody out. "I'm going to tell my parents tonight. They're going to go postal." And they would. But it was a caring postal, and it would pass eventually and they would be there for her and for the baby.

His lack of response prodded her to add, "Oh, I'm not going to tell them about you. They'll ask who the father is — duh — but I'll refuse to answer. I won't drag you into it."

"No. You won't drag me into it."

He stood and reached out his arms to her.

And she didn't want his embrace. She just wanted to leave.

146

She stood, too.

"I have to go now."

And he said again, in that same parroting tone, "Yes, you have to go now."

It wasn't until Howie Witherspoon took hold of her wrist instead of her hand that Hayley Norman felt fear.

She tried to pull her arm free and he held on, and then her fear ballooned inside her until it filled her whole soul.

No longer the raging emotional terror that he would leave her, that she would be alone again. Now she was afraid he …

She glanced to the left, to the cliff face.

So did he.

A little peep of a scream escaped her.

And he actually smiled.

"No!" The word exploded out of her throat on a breath of terror.

He held firm to her wrist and took a step toward the ledge only a few feet away.

From that moment on, Hayley Norman operated on pure instinct. Survival instinct. She didn't plot out a defense strategy or escape plan, she just lashed out. She reached out with her free hand and clawed his face, her perfectly manicured nails ripping four gouges down his cheek. He yelped in pain and she drew back her Army-boot-clad foot and kicked him in the shin as hard as she could, the leg with the bad knee, and it folded up. He went down to his knees but still held onto her wrist, wouldn't let go, so she kicked out again, blindly, just to get him to loosen his grip, not a targeted blow. But it caught him right in the face, a savage blow from an army boot. She could feel and hear teeth breaking and he released his hold on her arm and howled out a strangled, garbled cry of pain.

She turned and ran. He was between her and the

parking space so she couldn't make for her car. All she could do was run away in terror through the trees.

Her flight was wild and panicked, racing through the dense woods, dodging around bushes. No destination in mind, just the blinding terror in her chest that propelled her forward.

He had been planning all along to commit murder.

Dear holy mother of God, Sugar Bear — Howie Witherspoon— intended to push her off the cliff. He was going to *kill* her.

The thoughts didn't connect logically in her head but the general gist was all she needed anyway. *That* was the reason he'd wanted to meet her here. Not because he was sentimental about the first place they'd made love. Not for nostalgic, romantic reasons, to tell her goodbye, maybe make love to her one last time, tell her he loved her and would wait—

No. He had made their meeting here because he intended to shove her off the Scott's Ridge Cliff. How could …? Why would …?

Toby Witherspoon's words floated up inside her from the depths of her memory. The little boy had asked God to make his father stop hurting his mother. *Hurting his mother.* Howie Witherspoon was a violent man. Why couldn't she have figured that out from the terror on his son's face whenever she saw him? How Toby cringed away from him, went stiff when Howie hugged him. She had seen all that, noted all that and then categorically refused to make the mental connections that the clues implied.

Howie had been abusing his wife and maybe even his son for years. He wouldn't shrink from hurting her — he'd had lots of practice hurting people.

Hayley stumbled over another root, clumsy in the army boots. The root was snaking out from the trunk of a big oak tree and she almost went down, caught herself on the trunk and stopped, panting, crying, too, though she couldn't feel herself crying.

Over the hammer blows of her heart banging in her chest so hard she could see the Eastern Kentucky University tee-shirt logo move with each beat …

Over the ragged panting of her breathing that rasped painfully in her throat …

Over the loud buzzing sound that now filled her ears …

She could hear him. Freezing, she held her breath.

He was coming through the trees behind her.

Chapter Twenty-Six

It was going to sound crazy, Charlie knew. But she couldn't let everybody leave without saying anything. She and Sam and Malachi had agreed. It was important.

"I wasn't supposed to be the one to say this," she stammered. "It was supposed to be Malachi."

"My Malachi?"

Viola pulled the attention back to the stage. She looked genuinely surprised.

"Yes, Malachi—"

"He didn't never mention to me he's planning on giving a speech."

Charlie didn't know how to respond to that. Malachi had been spending a lot of time at the hospital with Sam and Charlie. She didn't know what he ordinarily did with his time, but surely he had been spending less of it with his mother than he had been since the Jabberwock.

"He and I and Sam … we've been talking, you know, trying to figure it all out. The Jabberwock."

Charlie realized as she spoke that she had been put in

her place. That Viola had re-established herself as the person in charge, the person who was to be listened to. Instead of addressing the crowd, Charlie was answering Viola Tackett's questions. Like a good little girl.

She resolutely turned to speak to the others in the room.

"We can't leave here tonight without talking about something more important than whether or not somebody's hay rake got stolen."

"Ain't nothing more important than establishing peace and order among ourselves. The nowhere people got to stick together."

That hit Charlie like a drop of water in hot grease.

In one sentence, Viola had set up an us-versus-them mentality. Viola and everybody else in the room was us and Charlie was them. Well, that wasn't going to happen.

"Don't make it sound like I'm some outsider, some flatlander from away from here," she snapped in a tone she suspected was not used often with Viola Tackett. "I grew up here. My mama was Sylvia Ryan. She made pottery, bowls and ... she gave ceramics classes."

She had to establish some street cred.

"My daddy left Nower County in 1967 for Vietnam and never came back. Missing in action. Killed in action. We never knew. But the three of us, me, my mama and my sister Mallory made our lives right here in a house at the foot of Little Bear Mountain."

Though she wasn't looking at Viola Tackett, she could feel displeasure pulsing off her in waves.

"I'm nowhere people, same as you."

"Where you been all these years?" Viola said, feigning simple curiosity, but Charlie was quickly learning that the dumpy little woman with the big bun of black hair — who was still holding a rifle on the crowd — didn't do or say anything that didn't push forward her own personal agenda.

"You don't stop belonging to the club just because you move away," she snapped, and would not look at Viola Tackett — aware that a look from Viola right now would cause internal bleeding.

"We are all in this together whether we like it or not because not a mother's child in this room can get past the borders of Nower County, no matter how important you are" — she looked at Sebastian Nower — "or how powerful you are." She did not look at Viola Tackett but she was sure the meaning was not lost on her. "Or how famous you are out there in the wide world."

Only a handful of people knew Charlie was really the bestselling children's novelist C.R.R. Underhill, but she would wager Viola knew it, because she didn't imagine there was much that went on in this county that escaped her notice, even if she did live in a log cabin on a mountainside out past Killarney, without a phone or indoor plumbing.

"We're stuck here together — but that's *not* the worst of our problems."

There was a murmur in the crowd.

"What's happening here … it's more than just a mirage you can't cross or you end up puking your guts out in the Dollar General Store parking lot."

"How do you know—?"

And Charlie actually cut her off.

"I don't *know*. None of us knows. But I will tell you what we have seen and what we understand — Malachi, Sam Sheridan … and," she choked up and had trouble getting the words out through her clogged throat, "Liam Montgomery and I have seen things maybe the rest of you haven't. Or if you have, you didn't take any note of them. Or pretended you didn't see at all."

"What things?"

"Old houses."

"They's lots of old houses in Nower County, empty that somebody moved out of" — Viola said the rest with a sneer — "to go live somewheres else."

"Oh, come on, you know I'm not talking about that." The words sounded dismissive and disrespectful — and that was just fine with Charlie. "I'm talking about the old houses that just got old, the ones that looked like yours one day and the next day they've aged a hundred years. You've seen them, don't tell me you haven't."

The crowd was silent then. Even Viola Tackett kept her mouth shut.

"Don't you wonder what happened to those places?"

"Do *you* know what happened to them?"

"No, not exactly, but—"

"Well, if you don't know what you're talking about why are you taking up our valuable time—?"

"I know what's happened to the people who used to be in those houses." She let that soak in before she continued. "And so do you."

She made eye contact with Betty Ann Gribbins, who'd either paid Bobby Joe Mattingly for a bunch of chickens or hadn't. She looked at Bobby Joe and his wife, Norma Jean, who had a strawberry birthmark covering one whole side of her face. Bobby Joe looked away, Norma Jean looked scared.

She looked at Thelma Jackson, who'd taught history at the high school and Thelma met her gaze straight up and held it for a beat. Gave a little nod, too, or maybe Charlie imagined that part.

She looked at Ethel Crump, who'd hidden from the

Jabberwock in her basement, Billy Dan Singleton, who'd lost his souped-up Chevy and Becky Sue Potter who might just have that baby right there on the auditorium floor.

"You know, you just don't want to look at it, don't want to admit it's real because if it is—"

"What are you talking—?"

"People are vanishing!" She cried out the words with emotion that might have sounded like weakness, or hysteria, but she couldn't help it. "Abner Riley, Harry Tungate, Reece and Cissy Tibbits and their girls, Sue-Sue and Patty. There are more, a lot more I don't know about, but those half-dozen are enough. One minute the house is here, and folks are fixing breakfast, and the next minute the house is a falling-down, hundred-year-old shack and the people are … *not there.* Vanished."

"What is it you're trying to say—?"

Charlie whirled on her and the fire in her eyes matched Viola's spark for spark.

"What I am saying — that *your son,* Malachi, was going to say here tonight — is that it's not enough to kick back with a beer and go on with life just like you've always done."

"Why ain't it—?"

"Because you're *wrong.*" She literally spit the words out at Viola, then turned and said the rest to the crowd. "About two very important things."

She held up one finger.

"You think the Jabberwock's going to go poof in a puff of smoke and be gone when you wake up in the morning and then you can go on up to Lexington to get new tires for your truck or over into Beaufort County fishing."

She shook her head.

"That's not true. It's pie-in-the-sky wishful thinking. Daydreaming. The Jabberwock didn't blow in here with the storm. It's not some meteorological phenomenon, some explainable freak of nature that'll work itself out. "

She held up a second finger.

"And you think that even if the Jabberwock doesn't leave, even if it keeps you locked up here, all you gotta do is figure out how to put food on the table, maybe drink a little shine now and then or smoke some weed, which really isn't a bad life, not all that different from how you were living before J-Day ..."

"And *you're* saying ...?"

"That's *wrong*. All of it. The Jabberwock isn't going anywhere because it isn't a thunderstorm or a tornado turned wrong side out. It is a *being*. It has a will. A purpose."

Nobody spoke after that, not even Viola.

"This is bigger than just figuring out a way to get along with each other." She cast a pointed look at Viola Tackett that she suspected earned her a permanent spot on that woman's bad side. And that was not somewhere anybody wanted to be.

"It's not just that we can't leave! That's not all of it. As we stay here, we vanish. It's happening right now. The Jabberwock consumes us, we cease to exist. You can't just sit back and make do with a life that ends at the county line. You better get up off your backside and start trying to figure out how to fight something that's going to eat you while you sit there."

You could have heard a mouse tiptoe across a cotton ball in the room.

"All of us are smarter than any one of us. We've got to figure this thing out — *all of us*. Together. Or the Jabberwock will pick us off one at a time until it gets us all. And we will vanish ..."

Her voice lowered, not just for effect but because she

had suddenly run out of enough air to finish what she had to say in a normal voice. "… just like Gideon did."

Chapter Twenty-Seven

The black frame had returned to the edges of Malachi's vision, the one that had formed when he was on the other side of the world, the one that only left him occasionally, when he was working with the others at the Middle of Nowhere, when he was …

What?

Engaging with the world? Was that all it took? Get out there and make nice with folks, go to a few parties maybe, ask a girl to dinner … in other words, get on with life. Did you just have to decide that's what you were going to do and the black frame would go poof in a puff of smoke, wouldn't continue to close in on your vision until you could only see the world through a small hole formed in it? And when it closed up altogether, you couldn't see the world at all.

No, that wasn't right. You saw the world. It just wasn't the real one out there beyond your fingertips. It was the one that only existed in your head, the world of horror and blood and death.

Malachi grabbed his thoughts, understood that he was

perilously close to the point that he'd be shoved out of the driver's seat of his own life and his own reality, and taken on an all-expenses-paid vacation into hell.

Focus.

"Malachi."

The word seemed to come from a long way off, like at the bottom of some very deep well. But it was just Roscoe, driving his truck toward Harry's house, desperate to find out what had happened to his twin brother.

Malachi knew Harry was gone, though. Roscoe probably did, too, but you had to try, had to look. You couldn't just accept that *uh oh, here's another one*. Somebody who was walking around in the sunshine yesterday — gone, poof, vanished. You couldn't just take that and move on.

But what could you do? In the face of something like that, what could …?

Something. Anything. Everything was preferable to nothing at all.

Harry's little house was at the bottom of a rise, with Dragon Root Creek running past it not fifty yards from the house. Malachi wondered if the house had ever flooded because the creek was such a close neighbor. He doubted it. Flooding in the mountains wasn't a common problem because flooding was caused by a creek backing up and creeks here ran straight down the hillsides, carried their water out into the flatland. Once there, if something got in the way, a creek would back up then, spread out of its banks and into the yards, basements, even the second floors of some houses.

Mountain folks had a saying for when the creek was full and running fast: "Creek's a'rushin' out there to defile the flatlands." Or they'd say, "pee runs downhill, too."

As soon as Roscoe passed the stand of trees that blocked the view of Harry's house, Roscoe cried out.

"No ... noooooo!"

Malachi had only been to Harry Tungate's house once, and that was when he was a little boy, come to ask did Harry mind if he and his brothers went hunting in Harry's woods. There'd been rumors that somebody'd spotted elk in the northern part of the county and the Tackett boys wanted to bag one if they could. Asking was just a courtesy. Harry didn't own the woods around his house. He owned the little plot of land where he raised a small amount of tobacco and Malachi suspected an equal amount of weed, had a garden and apple trees and the standard menagerie of farm animals, chickens for eggs, a milk cow, sheep, pigs and guinea hens. It was just a thing you did so a man wouldn't suddenly hear the sound of gunfire nearby and rush out into the woods packing.

Just that one visit hadn't printed a vivid image of the house in Malachi's mind but it didn't matter what it'd looked like then. Now it was a collapsed shack that barely resembled a house at all.

Roscoe roared down the hillside to the bottom, popped the clutch to kill the truck, leapt out and went running toward the pile of rotted timber, calling out, "Harry, Harry, where you at? You answer me, now, you hear. Harry!"

Then he started digging through the pile of rubble, calling out his brother's name in a ragged voice that hardly seemed human. The way you'd do after an avalanche, frantic to find your loved ones buried in the snow. Malachi got out and joined Roscoe, but didn't dig, just stood there beside the thing that was not a house anymore. Feeling the cold pulse off it like heat pulsed off a potbellied stove in the dead of winter.

"Malachi, come on. Help me dig. Help me find him."

"He's not here," Malachi said as kindly as he could. As soon as he had begun to feel the cold from the house, that felt like the draft of icy air that had belched out of Abner Riley's house, the black frame around his vision began to expand. Getting thicker and thicker. Pulling him inward away from reality. Sucking him down into the black depths of his own soul.

When Roscoe spoke, his voice was anguished, each word a separate pain. "If'n you ain't gonna help, go on — get back in the truck."

The black frame slammed shut with a bang in front of Malachi's nose.

"GET BACK IN THE TRUCK, SOLDIER," *Sergeant Moretti says.* *"We're pulling out."*

Malachi can't believe even Sergeant Moretti could be that heartless.

"Sarge, we can't leave now. They won't do anything as long as we're here, but as soon as we leave ..."

Malachi's squad is on a dirt road beside a cluster of houses, just outside Kigali, where the small contingent of American soldiers are stationed, tasked with guarding the airport, keeping it open so that evacuations of nationals from France, Belgium and other European countries can continue.

"That's not our problem," the sergeant said, then spouted the phrase he had used dozens of times, a phrase that said a whole lot more than the words. "Not our circus, not our monkeys."

A lame attempt at humor to cover up the fact that the man's a racist. As long as he is charming, his disregard for the lives of the black civilians here isn't so obvious.

There are probably two dozen people, clustered from all the houses into the one on the end by the road. The men, women and children belong to the Tutsi tribe fleeing in terror from the machete-wielding Hutus, who for weeks have been systematically butchering every Tutsi tribal they can lay hands on. Roads all around the airport are lined with piles of their corpses.

A band of about ten Hutus have found the terrified civilians, and would already have swarmed into the house and butchered every occupant, were it not for the presence of the squad of American soldiers who happened to pass by. They are unwilling to display their savagery before onlookers, so they are waiting for the Americans to leave before they slaughter the families huddled in the house.

The leader of the Hutu tribals is a tall gaunt man with a fat scar slicing across his left cheek and down his neck to his bare chest. His teeth have been blackened by chewing the narcotic weed khat, a shrub with leaves that contain a compound with effects similar to those of amphetamines.

The drug is rampant in Somalia, its addicts termed "skinnies' by American soldiers because the drug hypes them up and dulls their appetites, making them walking skeletons. Scar-Face and the rest of his crew look like chipmunks with wads of khat stuck in their cheeks. Saliva slowly breaks down the compound and the drug enters the bloodstream, while users spit on the ground a green confetti of discarded leaves.

Their eyes are wild. They carry bloody machetes and butcher knives. One has only a sharpened stick stained brown with blood.

"You go," Scar Face calls out. "Not your business."

At that moment a woman bursts out the door of the house and runs toward the American soldiers. She carries a baby and is dragging a little boy of about eight by the hand.

"Take my children," she cries at the soldiers. "Save them."

Scar Face gets to her before she reaches the road, raises his machete and buries it in her back and she staggers forward several steps with it stuck there. Sharp-stick man is one step behind and he spears the infant that falls out of her arms when she tumbles to the ground.

But the little boy is quick, and he darts away from the murderers *and makes it to the contingent of soldiers on the road, throws himself at them, grabbing hold of Malachi's leg and hiding behind it.*

Scar Face advances, machete raised.

Malachi isn't even aware of raising his weapon, sighting in on the chest of the advancing Hutu, doesn't even will himself to speak, as he calls out, "Touch this child and I will blow a hole in your chest big enough to drive a Humvee through."

Malachi's sergeant wheels on him.

"I said, get in the truck, Tackett. Leave the boy and load up."

Malachi doesn't move.

"That is a direct order, soldier. Get in the truck."

The Hutu takes a step toward him and Malachi fires, his bullet catching the man in the chest and knocking him backward. He throws the machete at the child as he falls and it catches Malachi in the leg, slicing him open from knee to ankle. Before the man hits the dirt, Malachi has swung the rifle toward the others in the man's crew, daring them to approach. "One more step and I'll—"

The world goes black.

When Malachi again opens his eyes, he is lying on his back in the transport truck, bouncing along the road toward the airport. His best friend, Charlie Blinkhorn, is leaning over him.

"I'm sorry, man, but I had to do it. You woulda shot all of them."

The man sitting next to him nods toward the front of the truck where the sergeant is sitting beside the driver. "But just one ... Sarge is gonna say the guy attacked you and you had no choice but to shoot him."

Malachi's mind is spinning and he is so dizzy he can barely manage to keep his head up. He hears what the man is saying, but the words aren't yet connecting to reality in his mind.

The boy. Where is the boy?

He tries to rise.

"I got to get back to the boy," he says, as hands restrain him and push him back down onto the floor. Malachi fights with all his

strength, which is no strength at all. His mind is caught in a loop. He has to get to the boy, find him, save him.

"Let me go. The boy—"

"Is dead, Malachi," Blinkhorn tells him. He pauses, sees Malachi still isn't tracking, and leans close to whisper into his ear. "The one with the sharp stick, he gave Sarge the little boy's head and told him to give it to you."

Then Malachi falls into another blackness, a different blackness.

MALACHI TURNED from Roscoe Tungate and started toward the woods.

"Harry ain't in the woods," Roscoe tells him. "He's here, under here. I know he is. Help me get him out."

"The boy," he said. "I have to find the boy."

Then Malachi broke into a dead run toward the trees.

Chapter Twenty-Eight

The big crowd of people had dispersed after the meeting, quietly going out to their vehicles and driving away. Charlie had no idea if they had bought what she was selling or not. Before the crowd left, Viola did her best to discredit Charlie.

"Nowhere people ain't like the rest of mountain folk. All mountain people got their own music, their own licker, their own dances, their own way of courting and their own way of thinking. But nowhere people are different from them folks. We're the people the rest of the world forgot. We don't matter — shoot, nobody even knows how many of us there are because we ain't even worth sending somebody out to count noses. The world's done passed us by. This Jabberwock thing, all it done was build a fence around us. It didn't change who we are. We're nowhere people and we look after our own."

She had glared at Charlie then, a look that both threatened and challenged. A look that said, "Go ahead, underestimate me — that'll be fun."

"We don't need some know-it-all who's spent more time away from Nowhere County than she ever spent in it, to fill our heads with a bunch of hooey about people vanishing. Going poof, like a puff of smoke. Like they's something out there trying to 'eat us up.' Them's scared stories for around the campfire but they ain't real life. There's plenty of real stuff to be scared of. Are you gonna have enough to eat? Will there be heat this winter? Water? What're we gonna do when we run out of gasoline? Ammunition? Them's real scary things, not made-up ones. You can leave here assured that I got this, I got answers to all the *real* questions. I ain't been chasing my own tail around looking for the boogeyman under the bed these past two weeks. I been figuring out how we all gonna *survive*."

One final glare.

"And we are gonna make it, without no help from you, missy."

Viola was just as hostile to the people who wanted her to return their weapons, the ones her sons had collected after she'd disarmed the crowd. "You got guns to hunt with. You don't need these here and you ain't getting them back until I decide to give them back."

As the crowd thinned, it became clear not everybody was leaving.

Duncan Norman and his wife, Miriam, stayed. The reverend had ash-gray hair cropped "high and tight" above a lean, ascetic face with a hawk nose and heavy eyebrows better suited to intimidating scowls than to smiles. He was tall and scarecrow thin, his wife was birdlike, too, and fragile. That the two of them had produced an offspring like the enormous teenager who'd sat blind and deaf in the Dollar General Store parking lot on J-Day gave credence to Charlie's long-held suspicion that the incidence of gypsies switching babies might be more prevalent than most people believed.

Lester Peetree, the hardware store owner who'd taken the kiln door off its hinges, stayed, too. So did two women Charlie didn't know, along with Hank Bayless, whose pickup had been used to haul away Willie Cochran, the Jabberwock's first fatality.

"We'll have to take Liam, his body, to …" Sam was trying to get her emotions in check enough to think clearly, but it was clear to Charlie that Sam's circuits had fried.

"To Bascum's," said Rev. Norman, who had knelt beside Sam. His voice was surprisingly kind and gentle, and Charlie readjusted her assessment of "severe." He looked up at Lester Peetree, who took the handoff.

"We'll see to it," Lester said. He and Hank Bayless lifted Liam up off the floor and carried him out of the building, dripping blood off the back of his shirt, and put him in the bed of Hank's pickup truck. It was only a couple of blocks to the funeral home and Mrs. Throck-morton kept Merrie occupied chasing fireflies in the dusk so Charlie could go with Sam and the others. They unloaded Liam's body, carried it into the basement, placed it on the tray in one of the mortuary's "body drawers" and slid the drawer into the wall.

It wasn't the only body in a drawer. Martha Whittiker rested there, too.

The others left. Sam and Charlie stayed behind, reluc-tant to go.

"What are we going to do?" Sam asked.

Charlie noticed more and more often that Sam was thinking the same thing she was, that the bond of two little girls who played baby dolls in the shade of the old elemen-tary school building had reconnected the women they'd grown to be.

"About a service and a funeral?" Charlie said. She put her arm companionably around Sam's waist. "We'll figure that part out."

"Okay." Sam let out a breath that was somewhere between a sob and a sigh. "You're right. The rest will have to wait until later."

"What rest?"

"What we do about Viola Tackett."

"She's clearly on the move to take over the whole county, but I don't know what you and I can—"

"Not that," Sam said. "You weren't where you could see. I was."

When Sam turned toward Charlie, Sam's face was as hard as granite.

"The bullet hole was in Liam's back. His *back!*"

Charlie's mind stumbled, trying to figure out what that meant, the implications—

"He'd jumped down off the stage and weighed into the crowd and then — *bang!* I was looking right at him ... could see *past* him."

When Charlie got it, her eyes caught Sam's and hung.

"And the person *behind Liam* ... was *on the stage.*"

Sam nodded. Her husky voice seemed almost to growl. *"Viola Tackett."*

Chapter Twenty-Nine

Run.

Hide.

Which?

Hayley was too panicked to make a rational decision, but the decision was made for her when terror propelled her forward, thrashing through the woods and the undergrowth. Between gasping breaths that exploded out of her chest, she heard someone running through the woods with the same abandon as she had. Howie was behind her, chasing her.

It was impossible to run fast in the clunking army boots and they made her clumsy so that she tripped over a tree root and sprawled on her belly in the leaves and dirt. Scrambling to her feet, she hunkered down behind the tree trunk, trying to get her breath.

Howie was a wild man. He wasn't just chasing her. He was yelling, screaming, howling in pain. Garbled words rode his screams. Obscenities. Threats. Anger … *rage!*

There was blind hate in the voice screaming out of the

throat of the man whose child she carried "beneath her heart." If he caught up with her, he would kill her.

Even without the bulk of the army boots, Hayley couldn't run fast. She was a hundred— okay, a hundred-fifty pounds overweight and she couldn't move fast no matter how hard she tried, not hauling all that weight around.

But Howie had a bad knee. He couldn't run fast on it or it would fall out from under him.

Could she outrun him if he saw her?

She didn't know—

And then she found out.

He had changed direction, had spotted her behind the tree and was coming right at her,

"Arrgggg, you whore. I'll kill you."

Hayley bolted, trailing the raging man and his screams behind her like the tail on a kite.

Now that he'd spotted her, she couldn't get far enough ahead of him, couldn't run fast enough to get out of his sight and hide. She would have to escape him by outrunning him. And Hayley Norman didn't believe that was possible.

Her heart was banging so hard her whole face pulsed with each beat. She was slathered in sweat, her hair pasted to her forehead, her breathing rasping, gasping.

There was a stitch in her side that hurt so bad she could barely stand up, let alone continue to run. But she couldn't stop. No matter how bad it hurt, she couldn't stop. The trees in front of her seemed to be thinning out, and that would make it easier going. But it would be easier for him to see her, too. In the fading light, the shadows of trees had offered some concealment, but in the open—

Then she realized why the trees were thinning. Up ahead of her was a logging road. The woods were full of them. It would meander down to Crockett Pike, and the turnoff to the parking space in the woods. If she took the road it would literally become a footrace. Could she get down it, into her car and away before Howie caught up with her?

Or should she stay in the woods, veer off to the right or left, make it harder for him to keep up with her on that bum knee? If she could elude him for a while longer, it would be dark. If she could just stay out of his grasp that long, he would never find her in the woods—

A truck.

There was a pickup truck on the road. Hayley couldn't run anymore. The best she could do was stagger, her breathing a gasping wheeze, bent over the stitch in her side, but the truck was driving slowly, which was the only way you could drive on a logging road full of gigantic potholes.

Who could possibly be out here in the woods on a logging road at twilight?

She didn't care who it was, she had to catch them. Had to get in front of them before they passed by, flag them down, plead with them for help.

Now it *was* a race. Not only away from Howie behind her but toward the pickup truck ahead. If it made the next bend before she got out of the trees and onto the road where she could be seen, the driver would pass unknowingly by and she would have lost all chance to flag him down. She didn't have enough air to cry out for help. She just had to get to the road before the truck passed.

Had to.

Thirty feet now.

Twenty.

Fifteen.

She was going to make it!

Then she felt a hand on her shoulder. She frantically shook off the hand and lurched forward. But then Howie grabbed a handful of her hair, yanked her backwards off her feet. She flew through the air and landed in a bone-jarring heap on the forest floor.

She looked up then into his face and it was a ruined horror. She screamed, shrieked, cried out in terror at the top of her lungs. Except she didn't. She couldn't get in enough air to breathe, let alone scream. The sound she made, terror and rage, rang out only in her head.

Howie's mouth was nothing but a bloody gash in his face, pouring gore down his chin. His nose was broken and bleeding and four deep *cuts* slashed down his left cheek — more than mere *scratches*. Where she'd clawed him with her fingernails looked like he'd been mauled by a bear.

He stood over her, panting, spewing out a spray of blood at her as he gasped for air, trying to catch his breath. She rolled over, tried to stand, but he tackled her, literally leapt on her back and used his weight to crush her down in the dirt beneath him.

He was coughing, gasping in her ear, almost-words, obscenities, hatred. He moved enough to yank her over onto her back so that the gore of his face was dripping directly into hers. He clamped his hand over her mouth to keep her from screaming and she struggled in panic, couldn't get in enough air through her nose. So she bit him as hard as she could, got the side of his thumb in her mouth and bit all the way to the bone. She could feel it with her teeth. He yanked backward in agony, would have screamed if he'd had enough breath. She heard the truck approaching and shoved at Howie with all her strength, wiggling and kicking out with her feet and hands.

Off balance, he toppled off her to the right and she scrambled to her feet and staggered the final fifteen feet to the edge of the trees and out into the road. The truck had just passed, leaving a wake of dust in the air, but the driver would see her standing there, swaying in the road when he looked in his rearview mirror.

When he looked back …

If he looked …

But he didn't. The pickup truck turned the final bend at the top of the hill and disappeared.

She heard Howie behind her and she turned. He was making a sound that might have been laughter. He had a broken tree limb the size of a baseball bat in his hand. He swung it at her head. She tried to duck, but she wasn't quick enough.

Then the world went black.

Chapter Thirty

As Stuart bounced along the road on his way to meet Shepherd Clayton, he understood that he was traveling through more than space. He was traveling from one culture to a totally different one that appeared similar on the outside but was distinct and separate in every way that mattered. Oh, Charlie had told him about it, about how remote the hollows were in the mountains where she had grown up. About the people who lived there who never saw strangers and wouldn't welcome one if they did.

"The words on the calendar about Abby Clayton's graveside service — you're sure they were in Charlie's handwriting?" Cotton asked as he piloted the car around the hairpin turns with an ease that unnerved Stuart.

"Her handwriting slants backward. I've teased her about it, told her that her sentences looked like all the words were facing a strong wind. Charlie wrote that note."

"Which means …?"

"Yeah, Cotton, what does it mean? Clearly, Charlie was there, was *in that house* … sometime. She planned to go to Abby Clayton's graveside service."

"You think she knew Abby Clayton? There wouldn't be any reason I could see that they'd have crossed paths. Abby was an 18-year-old high school dropout who lived … you're about to see how far back in the hollow she lived. I bet the sun only shines here a couple of times a week."

Stuart bleated out a frustrated bark of not-laughter.

"This doesn't make any sense Cotton. None of it does."

Cotton glanced at him with a sympathetic look, and Stuart decided not to make any more odd sounds because he didn't want Cotton to look at him, to glance away from the road even for a second. It was darker here at seven-thirty than it was "out there on the flat," and the mountain roads seemed even more treacherous. Stuart realized there was no true sunset or sunrise here and that struck him as sad somehow and he didn't know why.

"You bump along through life with the world operating today the same way it did yesterday and the day before," Cotton said. "And you never think about the functioning of ordinary reality. It is what it is. And then one day reality jumps the rails and goes off in a whole new direction, and you're left standing there, stunned, wondering … what just happened here?"

"Where is my wife? My little girl?" Stuart ground the words out between clenched teeth. "This can't be happening."

Gratefully, Cotton didn't look away from the road when he responded this time, like maybe he didn't want to make eye contact. "I suspect they are wherever Thelma is. And where everybody else in Nower County is."

"And where's that?"

He did shoot Stuart a look this time and his voice was anguished. "I've spent the past two weeks banging my head against the wall trying to figure that out." He looked back at the road. "But according to what your wife wrote on that blackboard, Abby Clayton's not there anymore … wherever 'there' is. She's dead."

"Died … of what? And is that it, do you think? The houses that are suddenly old. Are the people who lived there … dead?"

Stuart could launch that out there into the air between them because Cotton's house and Charlie's mother's house were untouched. But what if they returned to them after they visited Shep and found them old, dilapidated? What did that mean? He shook off the thought — and yawned to pop his ears. Changes in elevation plugged Stuart's ears so severely it sometimes took him a whole day after an airplane trip to hear properly. The up and down of the mountains was driving him nuts.

The house where Cotton pulled over … it appeared that the ravages of time had eaten out its heart and left nothing but a shattered ruin behind. Cotton said it was inside that ruin that Shep and Abby Clayton had lived, that Shep had driven away from that house one morning to go to Lexington to stay with his newborn son overnight while his wife came home. The Claytons told Cotton that Shep'd about had to hogtie Abby to get her to leave her baby's side even for a few hours. Shep had wanted her to get a good night's sleep because the baby wouldn't likely let her get much rest for a while. She never showed up. And when Shep and his baby son came "home" without her, the ruin was what the man found sitting where his house had been.

No wonder he had lost it. How did you leave a normal house and come home the next day and find this and still keep all your marbles?

There was a battered old car with missing wheels in the front yard up on concrete blocks, so ancient and rusted it was impossible to determine the make or the model. The trunk lid was held down with a piece of wire, and one back window had a piece of cardboard duct-taped in place to cover where the glass was missing.

"His mama told me that when he got home and found his house like this, he started howling, and I don't have any trouble believing that. She said the sound went on and on, like nothing she had ever heard in her life. Then he'd turned and kicked in the back door of his brother's car, just stood there slamming his foot into it again and again."

"Surely, he hasn't been *living* here."

"The Claytons and the Letchers are big families spread out all over the mountains in Poorfolk and Sawmill Hollows, which bump up against the Beaufort County line. A handful of Shep and Abby's relatives — brothers, uncles, cousins — live on the other side of the line and nothing happened to them. Shep and the baby, name's Cody, have been staying at his parents' house. They have a double-wide trailer on the Beaufort County side of Sharptop Mountain. Not an ideal situation."

"I've never seen a trailer house I thought was an 'ideal situation.'"

It was possible more people in the mountains lived in trailer houses than in ordinary houses, at least judging from what Stuart had seen. You could see them perched on the mountainsides, with winding dirt lanes leading up to them he couldn't imagine would be passible in the wintertime. They all looked like they were affixed to the mountainsides with white stick pins — satellite dishes. Charlie had told him once the satellite dish was the state flower of West Virginia and he could see why that was.

"Shep's father has MS and is in a wheelchair and he has a handicapped brother who also lives there. But apparently, Shep gets up every morning and ignores the baby, just gets somebody to bring him here and he sits all day in the ruin. He'd probably just stay here if his people didn't come every day to take him home."

"His people." Charlie had called her family that, too.

"Some of them tried to stay with him, keep him company, but he told them all to go away, that he wanted to be alone. His mama said when they come get him, he doesn't argue, goes right along, then he gets up the next morning and comes right back."

Cotton took in a deep breath and opened his car door. "Let's go see if he's any more lucid than he was the last time I saw him."

He wasn't.

The roof of the house had caved in on one side, taking one wall on the front with it. It was not a structure that looked stable enough to venture into. Cotton led them around to the back where a part of a wall was missing forming an opening into the remains of a bedroom. The frame of a bed sat there, with a clump of rotted fabric and stuffing on top of rusty springs. Shep sat in a lawn chair, collapsible, that Cotton said Shep's mother had put there. Before that, he'd just been sitting on the floor.

Stuart's first impression of Shepherd Clayton was that he looked like pictures he'd seen of the people in Nazi concentration camps when they were liberated by the American soldiers. Not just that he was thin way past the point of being gaunt, with too-long dark hair hanging in his eyes. The resemblance was in the look on his face — blank and haunted, hollow-eyed and hopeless. Shepherd Clayton had looked into the abyss. And the abyss had looked back.

"How ya doing today?" Cotton asked and it took a moment for Shep to come back from wherever he'd been and focus on Cotton. It wasn't until then that he noticed Stuart. When he did, his look turned hard.

"Who's this? What's he doing here?"

"This is Stuart McClintock. You remember Charlie Ryan — she'd have been a lot older than you, but she went to school here. Stuart's her husband. Her mother was Sylvia Ryan, gave ceramics classes in her garage at the foot of Little Bear Mountain."

There was some recognition in that, like he at least had heard of Sylvia Ryan.

"He's black," Shep said, the tone of voice carrying with it his disapproval.

"I'm black, too," said Cotton, trying to turn Shep's remark from an insult into merely an observation.

"*You* didn't marry no *white woman*," Shep said. But even his bigotry was off, unfocused, somehow didn't sound genuine. It was like he was playing the part of Shepherd Clayton — who was a racist and would have said a thing like that — but in reality was somebody else entirely. "What's he want?"

"He's looking for his wife, too. Just like I'm looking for mine and you're looking for yours. We came out to talk to you because we thought we could help each other. If we put our heads together, maybe we could find—"

"I ain't trying to find nobody. I ain't looking for Abby no more. I found her."

Stuart's heart began to hammer in his chest. *Found* her? If Charlie's calendar was accurate, Abby had died and been buried more than a week ago. If Shep *found* her … was she dead or alive?

As if to answer his question, Shep said, "My Abby's fine."

"Fine?" Cotton's voice was strained.

"Just fine. She said she's doing alright where she is and

told me not to go poking around looking for her, that she'd come on back home to me and Cody when the Jabberwock was done with her."

"What's ... the Jabberwock?" Cotton asked, but Shep blew by the question and looked at Stuart.

"The Jabberwock told Abby he don't like it, folks sticking their noses into some'm ain't none of their concern. Folks who ain't got no right to be here in the first place."

"*Who's* the Jabberwock?" Stuart asked.

"Ain't none of your business!" Shep snapped and there was a light in his eyes, like somebody was home in there now. "You hadn't ought to cross the Jabberwock." His eyes were piercing. "You mess with him, he'll mess with you. And you'll wish you never set foot in Nowhere County."

There was an otherworldly creepiness to this conversation that far out-distanced the nature of the craziness they were discussing. And Stuart began to feel that "too closeness," the sense that there wasn't enough air in the room, though there was a hole you could drive a forklift through in the wall. But instead of being frightened of yet another display of Welcome to the Twilight Zone, Stuart felt a flash of anger.

"You tell Abby to give Mr. Jabberwock a message from me. Tell him I'm not going anywhere until I find my wife and daughter."

Shep just looked at him, but somehow his look shifted when he did, and when he spoke it didn't sound menacing. In fact, it felt like Stuart was having a real conversation for the first time since he got here. Shepherd looked up at him through the shock of dirty brown hair hanging over his forehead with amusement in his eyes, like somebody who has seen the dude warming up on the other side of the ring and knows you're about to get knocked on your can.

"A person hadn't ought to stay somewhere they ain't wanted, and don't nobody want you here. Not Charlie and Merrie. Not nobody. You best leave." His voice dropped to a whisper. "While you still can."

Stuart and Cotton were driving away from the crazy man in the ruins of a house and a life, before it registered with Stuart.

"How did Shepherd Clayton know my little girl's name is Merrie?"

Chapter Thirty-One

Howie Witherspoon grunted and cursed and sweated as he dragged Hayley Norman's body through the woods to the cliff.

He had expended a lot of energy in wild rage when he caught her, had beaten her body until it was totally unrecognizable with the stick he'd used to bash in her skull. Hit her again and again, dripping blood out his mouth onto her body.

And his thumb. It felt like she bit it off! She broke the bone, he was sure of it, but there was so much blood and it was too dark to see …

He could only imagine what his face looked like now. Scratched, broken nose … and she had broken off one of his front teeth, too, when she kicked him. He could feel the jagged edge with his tongue. What could he do? There wasn't a single dentist in Nower County. Recognition of his injuries, of how he must look, sent him into such a fury he almost stopped dragging her, wanted to pick up a rock or a stick and attack her body, beat her—

No, she was dead. And he needed all his strength to

drag the sow's fat carcass to the edge of the cliff and toss her over.

He hadn't played it right, should have sweet-talked her into standing with him at the edge of the cliff so one shove would have done it. He'd been looking forward to hearing her scream all the way down. But he'd shown his cards too soon. Unless the filthy pig had been lying, she hadn't told anybody but Sam Sheridan she was pregnant — and Sam couldn't tell anybody, he didn't think. Wouldn't that be a violation of privacy? And the ugly cow had *said* she had told no one who was the father of the baby. Yet. She'd have spilled it, though, sooner or later, and statutory rape was still a crime in Kentucky. He'd looked it up. The age of consent was sixteen *IF* the partner was less than five years older than the girl. He was more than twenty years older and she hadn't yet turned sixteen that first time. It was right before her birthday. Her pious preacher father wouldn't have rested until Howie was in prison for life.

Howie shuddered. Physically repulsed by the thought of having sex with the bag of blubber he was dragging along by her hair and one arm. It was her fault, of course. She'd said she was on the pill and he didn't have any reason to doubt her. Looking back, she might have stopped taking the pill and gotten pregnant on purpose, to trap him. That first time — she'd been crying and he did feel genuinely sorry for her, and he'd held her … the *feel* of her body aroused him. Certainly not the *sight* of it. A man could fall off into that pile of fat and never find his way out again.

He might acknowledge some partial responsibility for that first time but what happened after that first time was *not* Howie's fault!

She would not leave him alone. Called him, showed up at the Dollar Store, waited until all the other customers left, then tried to get him to have sex with her, rubbing up against him — right there in the store. Apparently the danger of discovery was part of the turn-on for her. She had called his house one time too many, though, and Edna got suspicious. And when that witch had a bur under her saddle, there was no turning her aside. She always wanted to play the victim, the "poor-me," and the victim points a wife got when her husband cheated on her — with an underage girl! — Edna could bank those and draw interest the rest of her life.

They'd got into it the night before J-Day, one of the worst fights they'd ever had. He'd beat the crap out of her while the wind from that creepy storm raged outside. But she kept coming. It wasn't his fault she was dead. If she'd just let it be … but no. Women were like that. All women, a bunch of fat whores the lot of them.

So then he'd had to figure out what to do with the body. He had been scared spit-less he'd get caught, and where he put her wasn't a good place to stash a body but he hadn't had any time to plan it out. Then the Jabber-wock had swooped in to save the day, solving all his problems. Howie had put it out there that Edna'd gone shopping in Richmond with her sister, got caught "on the other side." Bada boom, bada bing — game over.

The problem of Hayley Whaley, as the other kids called her, wasn't quite as easy. But if he could just get her gargantuan blob of blubber off the cliff, he'd be safe. She had asked Sam to perform an abortion and Sam had refused. Then Hayley would just disappear, would vanish. And by the time somebody stumbled over her rotting corpse a month or two from now, they'd figure she threw herself off the cliff in a fit of despair, a pregnant teenager, the daughter of a minister. Nobody'd question it.

So how was he to explain his own injuries? Claw marks

down the side of his face, his mouth a ruin? His thumb! By the time her body was discovered, he'd be healed enough nobody would connect his injuries to her death. He'd claim that … he had fallen, slipped and tumbled down a hillside.

But the blood all over him! He had beaten her and beaten her and … He had to get home and out of these bloody clothes before anybody saw him.

Toby. *Crap.* The kid was home. Grant Jeffrey's mother had surely dropped Toby off by now, and Howie had never dreamed he'd be gone so long the boy would come home to an empty house. Well, he was eight years old, for crying out loud. Surely an eight-year-old was old enough to look after himself for a couple of hours. But Toby would be there when Howie got home. Would see the state of his clothing and what the fat slob had done to his face. There wasn't any way to hide it.

Well, then, that's the way it was. He'd tell Toby he'd been in an accident and the blood was his, and he tell the kid to keep his mouth shut, not tell anybody what he saw. The kid would do what he was told; he had seen what his father had done to his mother so he knew better than to cross him. Toby'd be fine.

He had finally dragged the body out of the woods. With no flashlight in the dark woods, he had tripped twice and almost broke his own neck. He dragged the body to the very edge of the cliff, kinda balanced her on her side, then stood, spit on her and shoved the body backward with his foot. And she was gone. It was too dark now to see where the body'd landed but it didn't matter. You couldn't jump off the Scott's Ridge Cliff and survive, no matter where you landed.

Hurriedly cleaned up around the picnic table, scuffling the drag marks the body'd made in the dirt in front of the cliff. The floor of the woods was covered with leaves and sticks and crap. There'd be no discernible drag trail there.

There was just one more thing left to do. He went as fast as he could to the clearing where the people who came to the overlook parked their cars. Hayley's father's car was parked beside his own. Opening the driver's side door, he leaned in and picked up her purse, opened it and found what he was hoping was still stuffed inside. The envelop of money he'd given her to pay for the abortion. Having to scratch together that kind of cash on short notice was part of what had gotten Edna's panties all in a wad, part of what had started that last fight.

Last fight. He was rid of Edna. And Hayley. He'd even gotten his money back, but the price he had paid and would continue to pay was waaaay more than the fat blob was worth. She had hurt him bad. He'd determined not to look in the mirror of the car, to wait until he got home to see the damage. Rage washed through him and out the other side.

Right now, his priority was getting home without anyone seeing him, getting cleaned up and seeing to his wounds. And Toby, of course. The kid was supposed to be in bed by now, should be sound asleep. And if he wasn't … Howie would make him wish he had been.

Chapter Thirty-Two

As they left the collapsed house where Shep Clayton sat, an old pickup truck turned in the lane and Cotton waved at the driver. He waved back.

"Shep's brother," Cotton said, "coming to get him and take him back to his mother's house."

Cotton drove the winding mountain roads in the dark as confidently as he had done in broad daylight. The two were silent. Seen through the clear mountain air, the stars twinkled big as chunks of ice floating in the sea of ink above their head.

Neither of them asked the question out loud, but it was implied, printed in flashing LED lights on the silence.

Now what?

Stuart glanced up at the Big Dipper and remembered pointing it out to Merrie on the deck of their house in Clarendon Hills. A lifetime ago. Two.

"You can't leave, you know," Cotton said. "Can't go back to Lexington or get a motel room in Richmond. Wouldn't want you to come driving in here tomorrow morning intent on doing what we already did today."

Cotton offered the scraps of a smile. "Living in Groundhog Day is exhausting."

"Then where—?"

"You're welcome to stay at my house," Cotton said. "It ain't much, but I've accumulated the rudiments of existence over the last couple of weeks. I got a storage unit in Lexington where I keep my camping gear and I hauled a bunch of it here — sleeping bags, basic cooking utensils, that kind of thing. The cots feel like they're lined with rocks." He paused. "There'd be cookies baking in the oven five minutes after we walked into the house if Thelma were home to bake them."

Stuart wondered how many times it would take for the impossible to slam into him like a wrecking ball before he would no longer be surprised by it.

"A cot's fine," he said. "I don't think I'll be doing a lot of sleeping."

But he was wrong.

After a supper of bologna sandwiches in Cotton's kitchen, eaten in a dead silence that bespoke their preoccupations, Stuart settled himself down on a cot and tried to get comfortable. Cotton Jackson deserved a truth-in-advertising award. The cot did feel like it was lined with rocks. He didn't think he would get a wink of sleep, tossing and turning in discomfort, but he fell asleep instantly. And he dreamed.

HE'S WALKING *through fog or mist so thick he can see nothing, absolutely nothing. It seems like he has been walking for a very long time. Hours. Days maybe. Never getting anywhere. Never leaving anywhere. Just there in the mist walking.*

Then he hears the cries.

Someone's calling his name.

"Stuart, Stuart, where are you?"

It's Charlie!

"I'm here, right here," he calls out. Except he doesn't. He opens his mouth but no words will come out. Only a scream, a high-pitched cry that sounds like ripping sheets. A sound like the man on the road, Reece Tibbits, made before he disappeared. He clamps his hand over his mouth to stop the screaming but it goes on and on, and he's afraid Charlie is still calling for him but he can't hear her above the noise he's making.

He grits his teeth together with every ounce of strength he possesses, and still the sound comes from his throat, but it's not loud now, muffled by his closed mouth.

"Stuart, where are you? I can't find you."

He can hear Charlie's voice, much closer now and he almost responds to her, but knows if he opens his mouth he will only be able to scream. So he waves his hands around in the mist in front of him, the way you feel around for the wall when you're in a dark, unfamiliar room. Feels and makes grunting sounds of stifled screams, and listens for Charlie to call—

"Daddy! I'm scared, Daddy. Help me!"

Merrie.

He loses it then, opens his mouth and forms words on the howling scream, a distorted ghastly sound that he means to say, I'm coming, honey, *but which just garbles the words and sounds so terrifying even to his own ears that he is sure it would scare little Merrie to death.*

"Daddy, please, come get me. Dadeeeeee—"

Her cry is cut off abruptly. Like the scream of the man in the road.

"Merrie! Merrie." He thinks the words in his head but doesn't say them, because he is only barely able to hold his jaw shut to keep from screaming himself. He tries to run—

He stumbles over something in front of him. Bangs into it and tumbles to the ground. He rolls over, feeling the bruises on his shins and looks at the thing he tripped over. It is an oblong box made of wood, about four feet long and two feet wide and ten inches deep. He examines it. There is no lid, no clasp, no hinges, nothing but a box — but it is not a solid block of wood because he can see the seams where it is put together.

Suddenly, a stench emanates from the box that is so foul he falls back in dismay. A smell so unutterably gross he's afraid he will vomit and if he does he will choke to death with his mouth clamped shut to muffle his screams. Except he isn't screaming anymore. The sound that was forcing its way up out of him is gone.

He doesn't want to get near the box because it smells so bad. Then the smell becomes a color. The stench flows out into the mist, coloring it a putrid green, flowing out into it like a drop of ink into water until all around him is green and the smell is so bad he—

The top of the box begins to lift up. A lid there he had not seen is rising up off the rest of the box, pushed up by something inside. The stink increases by a factor of ten when the lid is lifted and Stuart turns aside and vomits violently, projectile vomiting, his stomach ejecting the contents with such force it comes out his nose and mouth, chokes and gags—

Except it doesn't. He's vomiting, but nothing at all comes out even though he heaves and heaves. He finally gets his breath back from not-vomiting and turns back toward the box. The lid is lying beside it and green smell-fog is foaming up out of it.

He should want to get away from the box, as far as he can get, but he doesn't. He wants to see what is in the box, has to see what's in it. He gets to his knees and crawls the few feet to the box and looks inside, where the green stench is so thick he can see nothing.

And then the stench is gone. What was making it is not. It is a decaying corpse, horrifying beyond any description, blisters on the skin, beetles crawling out the eye sockets. All that is identifiable is the hair. The curly black hair. On the little body in the box.

The eyes pop open and death is in their depths. Now, Stuart wants to scream but can't, sits frozen as the eyes look at him, and the

mouth that is only held together by dangling decaying tissue opens and
sound comes out.

"Daddy."

Then Stuart screams.

SOMEONE WAS HOLLERING, making a horror sound that jarred Stuart out of sleep so suddenly he sat before he even realized he was awake and came close to tumbling out of the cot onto the floor. The real-world scream that dragged him out of the depths of the green-fog horror sounded remarkably like his own dream screaming had sounded. He staggered to his feet, tried to run toward the sound and banged painfully into something—

He lurched into the hallway and threw open the door to Cotton's bedroom. He lay on the floor in a sleeping bag, tossing and turning, moaning now instead of screaming. He knelt on the floor and grabbed his shoulders, shook him hard.

"Cotton! Wake. Up."

His eyes popped open but he continued to thrash around for a moment before Stuart could see recognition and understanding dawn on his features. Then he sagged back into the sleeping bag panting.

Stuart sat down on the floor beside him.

"I don't know what you were dreaming …" He stopped, started again, his voice softer. "But I think I was dreaming the same thing.

"I shoulda told you about the nightmares," Cotton said, hanging his head. "Shoulda warned you."

"You have had—?"

"Started the first night I slept in this house. Four or five days ago they stopped. I thought maybe it was because I didn't leave the county during that time. I'd been going out every day, trying to get somebody to listen to me, but by then I'd given up. Tonight … I had another one. the worse one yet."

"What did you dream about?"

Cotton didn't answer at once. Finally said, "Dead bodies, I don't want to talk—"

"That's what I dreamed about, too," Stuart said.

"I think I know why the dreams stopped and then started again."

Stuart thought he did, too, but he let Cotton say it.

"I think they stopped because I quit trying to do something about the missing people."

"And they started again when you met me because—"

"We're trying to figure it out.

Stuart absorbed that. Whatever was going on here, it wasn't some random, mindless force that had … had done whatever it was that captured a county full of people. The thing Shep called the "Jabberwock" took action *in response to* what he and Cotton had done. Cause and effect.

Why *Jabberwock*? Where did the name come from? Who knew? He let it go.

He got to his feet and extended his hand down to Cotton.

"How about you make a pot of coffee."

Cotton took his hand and pulled himself up.

"You got it. Strong enough to trot a mouse across … because I am *not* going back to sleep."

"Copy that!"

Chapter Thirty-Three

Toby Witherspoon's father was covered in blood, but the boy wasn't supposed to see. It was all over him, his clothes were soaked, his hands. And he was hurt! His mouth was smashed and bleeding, maybe teeth were broken. Toby wanted to ask him what had happened, but he couldn't. Toby wasn't supposed to see. He wasn't supposed to be awake.

Toby was only eight years old and his bedtime was nine o'clock. But in the summertime it wasn't even dark outside at nine o'clock. And that wasn't fair! Going to bed when it was still light outside. Okay, it was technically dark but that was just the mountain's shadow. The sun hadn't yet set out there on the flat and the sky didn't have no stars in it at nine o'clock, was still just a dark blue, not black yet.

Of course, ever since J-Day, the stars weren't right anyway, even when the sky was black.

Toby backed up from that thought, went another way in his mind because to consider that what had happened to Nowhere County was of such magnitude that it was even able to change the stars in the sky, was to admit to a force and power that Toby Witherspoon could not conceive. Besides, he had worse problems than the Milky Way and the Big Dipper, problems right here in his own house to concern himself with.

He'd been obedient, had gotten ready for bed even though there was nobody here to enforce the nine o'clock bedtime rule, a rule that was … *cataclysmically* unfair. He liked the word cataclysmic. He'd learned it from the National Geographic show on television about a huge volcano that blew up, and made an effort to use the word in any conversation where he could insert it. Toby was what the other kids called a nerd and his mother had graciously called a bookworm. He read everything he could get his hands on — history books, the Bible, the Farmer's Almanac. His mind was a dusty attic full of all manner of random useless pieces of information — like the Prophets of Baal were consumed in a fire from God … and broccoli, cabbage and cauliflower were vegetables that'd survive a light frost.

His thoughts almost universally centered on his mother, Edna Witherspoon. About how badly his father treated her. And about where she was, why she didn't come home, what had happened to her.

Toby didn't want his mind to go there, but it was pulled there like those magnets in science class where Mr. Robertson flipped the switch on that great big battery and the pile of metal shavings was drawn all the way across the table to the magnet.

His worries about his mother were those little metal shavings. They were *everywhere*, so fine you couldn't see the individual grains, but when the whole pile was snapped instantly to the magnet, you could see them all. Her jacket in the closet, her house shoes still sticking out from under the bed. The drip of catsup on the kitchen floor that was still there two days after he spilled it because she wasn't there to wipe it up. His clothes in a wrinkled pile in the laundry room, not stacked neatly in the drawers of his dresser. Even his own face in the mirror. Especially when the mirror was fogged right after he took a shower, he could see his mother's features stamped on his own face. She wasn't beautiful, but she had blonde hair that didn't come out of a box and so did Toby. And she had large blue eyes framed by dark brows and Toby inherited eyes just like hers. Her mouth, too, the way her bottom lip stuck out a little bit, like maybe she was pouting. Toby's did, too.

Her perfume — the smell still lingered on her clothes hanging in the closet and sometimes when he was so lonely he couldn't stand it anymore, when it hurt too bad to breathe, he would go into her closet and stand among her shirts and dresses hanging down all around him and pretend she was just gone into the Ridge to the grocery store. She'd be right back.

Except she wouldn't.

And not because she was kept away by the Jabberwock, no matter what his father said. He had told people she had gone shopping with her sister on J-Day and everybody believed him and went on about their business as if there were no possibility that his father might be *lying* Lying because he had … done something. Toby didn't know what, wasn't sure he even wanted to know what, but he did know that his mother had not gone anywhere before J-Day. He had seen her that day, talked to her that day. Of course, when his father gave him that look and said, "Why son, you must be mistaken. Your mother went to Lexington shopping with your Aunt Wanda, don't you remember?" he had sense enough to agree, nod his head up and down in a "yes sir" like a good little bobblehead doll. But it wasn't true, not any of it.

Toby had gotten into his pajamas, dug them out of a pile of clean clothes on the floor in front of the dryer, not folded up neat in his dresser drawer. But he never had any intention of going to bed. How could he do that, just go to bed, go to sleep, when he was all by himself in the house and *he was so scared?*

His mother would never have left Toby alone. Not even during the daytime, much less at night. He was eight years old and tried to act tough, but the truth was that he was afraid of the dark and as soon as it started getting dark outside he wanted to cry, wanted his father to come home though he never wanted his father, never wanted to be anywhere near him, but when it got dark outside, Toby was so scared he wanted his father to come home because his father was better than nothing.

He didn't know where his father had gone, only knew that it was to meet somebody named Hayley but he wasn't supposed to know that. He'd overheard the name on the phone. He hadn't been trying to eavesdrop, he really hadn't, just heard the phone ring and picked up the one in the upstairs hallway at the same time his father answered it downstairs. Then, he couldn't hang it back up because it would make a clicking sound when he did and his father would know he'd been listening and he'd get in trouble so he just stood there with the receiver in his hand while his father talked, waited until after his father hung up to put it back in place.

His father had been mad at the Hayley person on the other end of the line, who might have been the fat girl who had taught his Vacation Bible School class a couple of years ago but he didn't know for sure. The Hayley person didn't appear to know that his father was mad, either, didn't recognize that hard edge in his voice that said you needed to make yourself scarce quick. She just blew through it. Toby had learned better. So had his mother.

"Hayley! Why are you calling me? I told you not to call me. What if Toby'd picked up the phone?"

"I'd have pretended it was a wrong number, or asked to speak to his mother and he'd have told me she—"

"I don't want you talking to Toby about his mother!"

"I wouldn't … why …? What's wrong with you?"

His father'd said there wasn't anything wrong with him but wanted to know what was wrong with her, if Sam somebody had agreed to fix it. But she wouldn't tell him on the phone, said her mother might catch her talking and he said he wanted to meet her, that he'd call her back and tell her where.

Toby'd come into the kitchen later as his father'd said "Scott's Ridge" into the phone and then hung up. He said he was going out right after that, so it must have been to meet the person on the phone. Toby had whined, a little. He knew it wouldn't do any good, would only make things worse but he couldn't help it.

"I don't … like to be here by myself. Please, don't go—"

His father had grabbed him by the upper arm, squeezed so tight it hurt and yanked Toby up so he could lean over and talk right into his face.

"Afraid of the Boogeyman, are you? Crybaby! Well, if you keep whining, I'll give you a reason to cry."

He had let go of Toby's arm, shoved the boy away, and left.

Dressed in his pajamas, Toby sat down to wait by the front window for his father to come home. Didn't leave the lights on in the living room like he wanted to because he'd get into trouble for wasting electricity. As soon as his father pulled into the driveway — he couldn't put the car in the garage because the ski boat was in there — Toby would bolt like a rabbit up the stairs and hop into bed and pretend to be asleep when his father came in.

Finally, car lights turned off the highway onto the lane where Toby's house was one of three houses. Two of them had been deserted for years, the third was old man Hayes who was almost deaf and could barely see, who always kept his lights on all night long. Toby waited until he could hear the crunch of the tires on the gravel driveway, was ready to run upstairs as soon as his father stepped out—

But when he saw his father, he froze. What had happened to him? When he started toward the house, limping that strange way he did because of his bad knee, the motion sensor light over the front of the garage came on and Toby got a good look at his father's face. His face looked like …

Like Toby's mother's face had looked that time when she accused his father of seeing a "prosecute." She couldn't go out of the house for a month, told people she had the flu.

Toby turned and bolted out of the room and up the stairs, wondering who had beat his father like his father beat his mother … and wishing he could have been there to watch.

Chapter Thirty-Four

Charlie drove home from the Ridge with Merrie sleeping soundly in the back seat, strapped in, not in a car seat. The car seat had been in the airport rental that vanished on J-Day. As her headlights reached out like twin light sabers into the darkness, Charlie realized that she had started crying again. Well, maybe not crying, not like she had done as she knelt beside the body of the young man who had been trying *so hard* to do his job. She wasn't making any noise at all now, but her shoulders were shaking and tears were streaming out of her eyes, down her cheek and dripping off her jaw.

Liam. Poor Liam. He'd wanted nothing in the world except to man up to the uniform he wore. He wanted to protect and to serve. And Viola Tackett had killed him.

What was it she'd threatened? "I'll shoot you down soon's I would a lame horse." She had done just that, shot him down in cold blood. Not so much as a blink.

And what were she and Sam supposed to do with that, *about that?*

Should they, could they tell Malachi? Malachi, whose

no-show had left Charlie and Sam to carry all the water — in a bucket that had a hole big enough to put a fist through. If he'd been there, people would have listened — because he was a Tackett, sure, but also because he was a returning soldier. Everybody knew that he had gone off to some war somewhere and had returned damaged by it. But he had, by golly, *gone*, he'd taken up arms and done his duty. Folks respected him for that.

But if Malachi had been there, what would he have done that she and Sam hadn't? What would …?

A sudden, horrifying thought hit Charlie so hard it stole her breath. Whose side was Malachi Tackett on? Was that the reason he hadn't shown up at the meeting — because he knew what his mother was going to do and he was in league with her and his brothers?

Charlie couldn't believe that, *wouldn't* believe that. Malachi was on their side, hers and Sam's. He was the one who was leading the charge to do battle with the Jabber-wock in an effort to save E.J.'s life. He wouldn't turn on them. Would he?

Actions speak louder than words, Charlie girl, her mother would have said. Point of actual fact, Malachi'd said he'd be at the meeting, would stand up there and tell everybody what the Breakfast Club had figured out. Would warn them, make sure everybody understood that the Jabber-wock wasn't some random circumstance to be endured but an enemy to defeat, a monster to kill before it killed you. But Malachi hadn't delivered the message. Charlie had done the best she could as a stand-in but it wasn't the same. Bottom line: Malachi Tackett had bailed.

Where had he been? What could he possibly be doing that was more important than coming to that meeting and speaking his piece? Would he really have stood up to his mother when she started her little power grab? His brothers? And what would Viola Tackett have done if her own son refused to dance to the tune she was playing?

Where was Malachi?

She and Sam had only briefly mentioned him. Charlie could see Sam didn't want to talk about it so she had let the subject drop. Sam was even more upset by Malachi's no-show than Charlie was. And it was possible she and Sam were yet again on the same wavelength, not wanting to say out loud the fear that had crept into both their hearts. Maybe Malachi had failed to show up because he had … *vanished.* Maybe he was just gone, like Abner Riley, Harry Tungate, Reece Tibbits and who knew how many others.

Maybe he had been … *taken,* snatched up into the jaws of the Jabberwock.

That's the way she thought about it now, like a creature with jaws.

Beware the Jabberwock, my son, with jaws that bite and claws that catch.

She had written eleven children's books about three little kids who did battle with dragons, using swords with magical powers to slay the beasts. She had made each of the dragons unique. Balderdash had been a huge red dragon with yellow cat eyes. Millicent had been a female dragon, smaller, black, with spikes on her tail and claws as sharp as knives. Constantine had been pure white, with red eyes that glowed like coals when he breathed fire.

Those images were metaphors in her mind for the Jabberwock, and eventually she would try to puzzle out in her mind the connection between her books about dragons and the real dragon they all faced. But not now, her mind was too fried to process any higher-order thinking.

She pulled into the driveway of her mother's house, her headlights sweeping over the huge fallen limb that had been torn off the tree by the storm. The one in the driveway that Merrie tripped over. Charlie had dragged it out into the yard and just left it there and thought every time she saw it that she needed to get a chainsaw, cut it up and ...

She got out, went around the car and opened the back door, unhooked Merrie from her seatbelt and lifted her up into her arms. The child was out cold, that deep sleep that had made it possible for—

Slam!

She banged the door shut on those thoughts. *Not tonight!*

Carrying the sleeping child up the sidewalk to the front door, she didn't even question anymore why that was, why she no longer went into the backyard through the gate and in the kitchen door. That's what kitchen doors were for. Front doors were for guests; back doors were for family, that's what her mother'd always said. Flipping on the light switch in the front foyer, she crossed the living room into the hallway and down the hallway to her bedroom, where Merrie slept on a day bed at the foot of her bed. She recoiled from the images that filled her mind, of another night when she had laid a sleeping child down on the bed, took her shoes off and ...

Not now, she pleaded with the rogue thoughts. Please, *not now!*

Slipping the child's shoes and socks off, she planted a kiss on her forehead and pulled the blanket folded on the end of the bed up over her. It was a light blanket, but it was all she'd need. It would not get down below sixty degrees tonight.

The realization that that was true made her nauseous. She no longer looked up into the night sky. At the random, unblinking lights that weren't stars. She didn't want to see. Stepping out of her own shoes, she slipped out of her clothes and into her light summer pajamas.

Her mind was so exhausted she couldn't think, yet thoughts spun around and around in it so fast they were in danger of catching her hair on fire. Both at the same time. Impossible? You betcha. Mutually exclusive processes operating together — piece of cake in the Jabberwock world.

Face washed, teeth brushed, she went into the kitchen. Too fried even to boil water for tea, she got a Diet Pepsi from the cupboard. The last can.

She turned to leave the room when her eyes fell on the chalkboard — where her mother had written the last item on her We're Not in Kansas Anymore TO-DO list — buy bird seed.

She thought of this morning, when she'd imagined she saw Stuart's handwriting there, had written some stupid message of her own in response.

Stuart.

She actually groaned out loud. She couldn't turn anywhere in her mind anymore without running into pain, like her whole brain was full of razor blades. With a little burp of sardonic laughter, she stepped to the chalkboard, picked up the piece of chalk from the tray and wrote, "I want to go home!"

She put the chalk back in the tray and looked at the words. Shaking her head, she reached for the eraser. And froze.

Her heart began to bang around in her chest like a sperm whale in a fish tank.

Words were forming on the blackboard below what she had written.

She wanted to run out of the room, but her body had staged a revolt, had mutinied and refused to obey her commands. Unable to move at all, Charlie just stared spellbound as … someone? Some*thing?* wrote beneath her plea.

The handwriting wasn't Stuart's. The letters were formed with big, bold strokes, as if the chalk used to write them had pressed down hard on the blackboard. Angry strokes, she thought. Not cursive, all caps, printed.

The words formed slowly, but were perfectly formed, distinct and legible.

Beneath where Charlie had written "I want to go home" were the words:

No! Stay here and play with me.

THE END

A Note from the Author

Thank you for reading *Trapped.*

If you enjoyed this book, you please consider writing a review on your favorite bookselling site so other readers might enjoy it too. Just a couple of sentences would mean a lot to me.

Thank you!

Ninie Hammon

About the Author

Ninie Hammon (rhymes with shiny, not skinny) grew up in Muleshoe, Texas, got a BA in English and theatre from Texas Tech University and snagged a job as a newspaper reporter. She didn't know a thing about journalism, but her editor said if she could write he could teach her the rest of it and if she couldn't write the rest of it didn't matter. She hung in there for a 25-year career as a journalist. As soon as she figured out that making up the facts was a whole lot more fun than reporting them, she turned to fiction and never looked back.

Ninie now writes suspense--every flavor except pistachio: psychological suspense, inspirational suspense, suspense thrillers, paranormal suspense, suspense mysteries.

In every book she keeps this promise to her Loyal Reader: "I will tell you a story in a distinctive voice you'll always recognize, about people as ordinary as you are--people who have been slammed by something they didn't sign on for, and now they must fight for their lives. Then smack in the middle of their everyday worlds, those people encounter the unexplainable--and it's always the game-changer."

Also By Ninie Hammon

Cornbread Mafia

Fire In The Hole

Blown' Up A Storm

Ridin' For A Fall

Nowhere, USA

The Jabberwock

Mad Dog

Trapped

The Hanging Judge

The Witch of Gideon

Blown Away

Nowhere People

Through The Canvas Series

Black Water

Red Web

Gold Promise

Blue Tears

The Taken Saga

The Taken

The Changed

The Hidden

The Saved

The Unexplainable Collection

Five Days in May

Black Sunshine

The Based on True Stories Collection

Home Grown

Sudan

When Butterflies Cry

The Knowing Series

The Knowing

The Deceiving

The Reckoning

The Fault

Stand-alone Psychological Thrillers

The Memory Closet

The Last Safe Place